PESTS

HODDER

HODDER CHILDREN'S BOOKS

First published in Great Britain in 2020
by Hodder and Stoughton

1 3 5 7 9 10 8 6 4 2

Text and illustrations copyright © Emer Stamp, 2020

A CIP catalogue record for this book
is available from the British Library.

ISBN 978 1 444 94962 9

Printed and bound in Great Britain
by Clays Ltd, Elcograf S.p.A.

The paper and board used
in this book are made
from wood from responsible sources.

MIX
Paper from
responsible sources
FSC® C104740

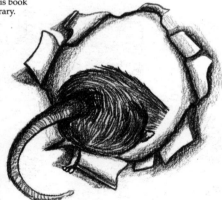

Hodder Children's Books
An imprint of
Hachette Children's Group
Part of Hodder and Stoughton
Carmelite House
50 Victoria Embankment
London EC4Y 0DZ

An Hachette UK Company

www.hachette.co.uk
www.hachettechildrens.co.uk

The PESTS Test

Answer these simple questions
to find out how pesty you are...

1. You accidentally poop in
the middle of the floor.
Do you:
A) Cry
B) Run away
C) Hide it

2. You find an expensive
cashmere jumper do you:
A) Stroke it
B) Wear it
C) Eat it

3. It's most dangerous to go
out in:
A) The middle of the night
B) Your underpants
C) Daylight

4. You are spotted by a
mans, do you:
A) Run
B) Wave
C) Play dead

5. What are you most
afraid of:
A) The dark
B) Monsters under your
bed
C) Nuke-A-Pest

Go to the next page
to see what the
results mean

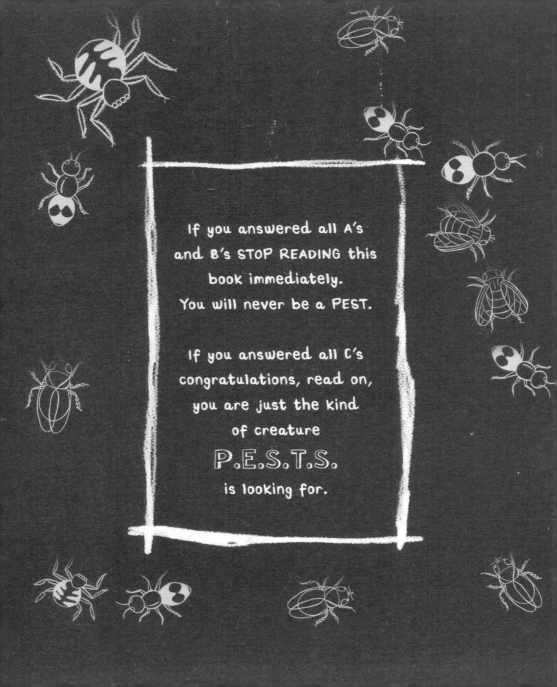

If you answered all A's
and B's STOP READING this
book immediately.
You will never be a PEST.

If you answered all C's
congratulations, read on,
you are just the kind
of creature
P.E.S.T.S.
is looking for.

ME!

This is me, Stix. I'm almost the height of an eggcup
(I've measured myself against lots of objects and this
is the thing that's the closest to my size).

I live in a nest hidden away behind the washing machine,
in the kitchen of Flat 3, Peewit Mansions. I know the exact
address because it's written on the envelopes
we sometimes shred up to make our home.

stix

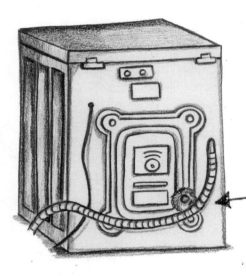

Our nest.
I live here
with my
grandma.

Grandma is VERY OLD. But we're not allowed to talk about exactly how ancient, because she says a lady mouse never lets on her age.

I did once, before I can remember, have parents. But we don't talk about them either. Whenever I ask what happened – how they died –

2

Grandma just shakes her head and says, 'You're not ready for that kind of information yet.'

I used to have a grandpa too. I can just about remember his face. It was old like Grandma's, only with a lot more whiskers. He died soon after my parents. Grandma said it was from a broken heart. But I don't think that's actually possible – whoever heard of a heart breaking!

Another thing Grandma says is that as a mouse you have to be smart.

A smart mouse, she says, gets to do as it pleases, gets to go where it likes and eat what it wants. A smart mouse knows how to go undetected. On the other paw, a silly mouse doesn't cover its tracks. A silly mouse gets seen. And as Grandma likes to say (often): 'a seen mouse is a dead mouse'. She also says:

A slow mouse is a dead mouse.

A greedy mouse is a dead mouse.

A noisy mouse is a dead mouse.

A stupid mouse is a dead mouse.

Sometimes I wonder how me and Grandma are still here. It seems staying alive is a hard thing for a mouse to do.

MY HOME

We share Flat 3 with a family of mans (that's our word for these funny-looking creatures) and their odd-shaped dog, **Trevor**.

Of course, apart from Trevor, they have no idea we live with them. I know he'd love to tell them all about us, but he can't speak mans. **Bad luck, Trevor!**

MyLove

Boo-Boo

Schnookums

Trevor

'There are mice living behind the washing machine.'

'I think he's trying to tell us that he wants a walk.'

To be fair, none of us creatures can speak mans, but at least we can understand it, and we can all understand each other. We're smart like that – much cleverer than those stupid mans who can only talk to each other!

The lady mans is called **Schnookums** and the man mans is called **MyLove**. They have a baby mans who makes **A LOT** of noise. Her name is **Boo-Boo**.

Grandma says there are good mans and bad mans. She says we're lucky, as we have very good ones. Apparently, some mice have terrible mans that clean all the time so there are no scraps to eat, or that never sleep so you can never sneak out at night undetected. But ours aren't like that. They:

1. **Only clean once a week - which makes the chances of finding food much higher.**
2. **Don't have a cat - Trevor is annoying, but he's never going to try to eat us.**
3. **Go to bed early - which gives us plenty of time to forage.**
4. **Have never called Nuke-A-Pest.**

The last point is VERY important. Nuke-A-Pest is the worst thing that could happen to us. Worse than the mans cleaning up every day. Worse even than a cat. Nuke-A-Pest is **BAD, BAD NEWS.** They know every possible way to kill us: traps, poison, gas. Grandma says, 'When they come, we go.' And by 'go' she means 'die'.

NUKE-A-PEST

Got a pest problem? Are you infested?
Time to call Nuke-A-Pest.
Traps. Poison. Gas.
We kill all pests DEAD. REALLY DEAD,
or your money back.
Call us TODAY and say GOODBYE,
VERMIN, FOREVER!

Though our mans have never called Nuke-A-Pest, they do have one of their ads stuck on their fridge. Grandma makes me read it every night so I always remember to be **EXTREMELY** careful.

Whenever we're looking for food, we always follow one VERY IMPORTANT RULE – Grandma is very strict about this. We never, ever leave any sign of what we've been up to. Grandma has another saying: 'Leave a trace, die in a trap'. By this she means if the mans get even the faintest whiff we're here they'll call the dreaded Nuke-A-Pest.

She says we must ALWAYS, ALWAYS, ALWAYS 'Keep It Tidy'.

The Four Rules of Keeping It Tidy:

1. **Never tear open packets.**
2. **Never chew holes in cardboard or plastic containers.**
3. **Never poop in places mans will see.**
4. **Never let your nails grow so long they scratch on the floor.**

I've had these drummed into me every day since I can remember.

So, all day we hide and sleep, tucked away in our little nest. Then, when night falls – once we're sure the coast is clear and the mans are fast asleep – we creep out of bed and down the back of the washing machine and out into ... the kitchen!

My grandma chose the washing machine to live behind because it's warm and it's safe (no mans ever look behind their washing machine) and, most importantly, it's near food.

9

The kitchen is where we find most of what we eat. We call it Zone 1. The mans we live with are rather messy (Grandma says they used to be tidier, but then Boo-Boo came along and made them too tired to clean), which means there's always yummy stuff to be found. You just have to know where to look.

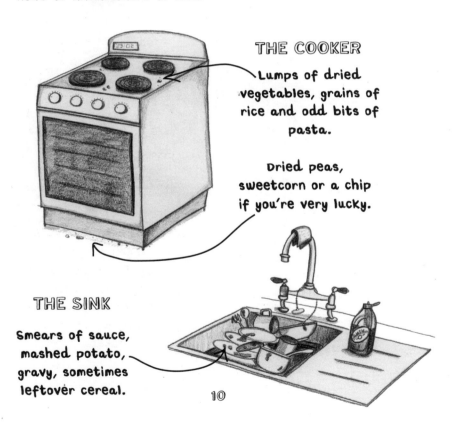

THE COOKER

Lumps of dried vegetables, grains of rice and odd bits of pasta.

Dried peas, sweetcorn or a chip if you're very lucky.

THE SINK

Smears of sauce, mashed potato, gravy, sometimes leftover cereal.

THE BABY MANS' CHAIR
(our favourite)

Lumps of rice cake,
crumbs of rusk,
hunks of breadstick,
bits of cheese,
chunks of sausage,
balls of mashed
potato ...

THE FRIDGE

Whatever has been
brushed underneath,
e.g. breadcrumbs,
peas, cubed carrot,
sweetcorn.

11

There's also a chance of food in Zone 2 - **the living room**. When the mans watch TV in the evening they like to eat biscuits. There are always crumbs to be found. Schnookums likes Custard Creams. MyLove likes Bourbons. Grandma likes the Custard Cream crumbs,

but I prefer the Bourbon ones, especially if they still have a bit of the chocolatey middle stuck to them.

Zone 3 is **the bathroom**. This is the most boring room in the whole flat. There's never any food in here. It's also the strangest room. When Grandma told me what a toilet was and how mans sit on it when they poop, I laughed so much I gave myself a stitch.

There's also this thing called a bath. Mans fill it up with water and then lie in it. Grandma says this is how they clean themselves. It seems like the most stupid thing ever. Mans' tongues are HUGE — why don't they just lick themselves all over like a normal animal?

Zone 4 is **the bedrooms,** which are upstairs. MyLove and Schnookums share one and Boo-Boo has the other. There's no food in here either. Well, unless the mans have had something called 'BREAKFAST IN BED'. But they have never done this in my lifetime. Grandma says they haven't done it since they had Boo-Boo.

Zone 5 is **the hallway.** This is where the mans keep their coats, shoes, MyLove's shiny green bicycle and Boo-Boo's pushchair (Grandma finds it very funny that mans need something like this to move their children around). We often find crumbs of food around its seat and in the bag that hangs underneath it. Sometimes we even find half-eaten snack bars.

At the end of the hallway is The Frontier Door. This is much bigger than the other doors in the flat, and on the other side of it lies ... The Beyond. I am expressly forbidden from ever going further than The Frontier Door. The Beyond is strictly out of bounds. Grandma says we have absolutely no need to go there, that we have all we need to survive right where we are.

Sometimes I wonder what it's like out there in The Beyond

– are there other little mice just like me? – but apparently only a greedy or a stupid mouse would go out into The Beyond, and we all know what happens to them!

And anyway, tonight is my **FAVOURITE** night of the week, the one I **REALLY** look forward to. Tonight it's PIZZA NIGHT. The mans always leave their pizza boxes stacked up by the rubbish bin. Whichever mans designed the pizza box is a GENIUS! They put a perfect mouse-sized hole in every one!

All we have to do is climb through the hole and, **BINGO**, we're in a world of soft, doughy crusts smeared with tomato sauce – and if we're lucky, a bit of cheese.

When we've finished eating, Grandma goes back to bed. She says her old bones need rest. But my bones don't feel old in the slightest. In fact, when night-time comes, I usually feel I could literally burst with energy.

So some nights ...

Like tonight ...

(Well, OK, most nights ...)

After

   she's

      gone

         to

           sleep ...

                   ... I sneak out of bed.

I mean, if I'm careful and follow all Grandma's rules, it's not like anything bad is going to happen to me, is it?

AFTER-HOURS
FUN!
FUN!
FUN!

The kitchen is very dark at night. Apart from the green glow from the clock on the cooker, there's no light at all. But this isn't a problem for me. Using my whiskers to feel and my nose to smell, I can find my way around easily.

Trevor, who smells like the dog food he eats (unless the mans have recently washed him in the bath, haha!), sleeps on a fluffy rug next to the fridge. It is very important

I don't wake him. A yapping Trevor would definitely wake the mans. To make sure he's properly asleep, I use a special technique I call the Trevor Whisker Tickle. Basically, I twang one of his nose hairs and if he doesn't stir, which he usually doesn't, I know I'm good to go.

I like to warm up with what I call my Stix Skills. I am very proud of these and am adding to them all the time.

My top six right now are:

STIX SKILLS:

1. Climbing up the leg of a dining chair. I can get all the way to the top. (The really fun bit is sliding all the way back down again.)

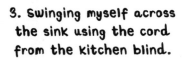

2. Swinging across the draining rack - my record is twelve back-to-back swings.

3. Swinging myself across the sink using the cord from the kitchen blind.

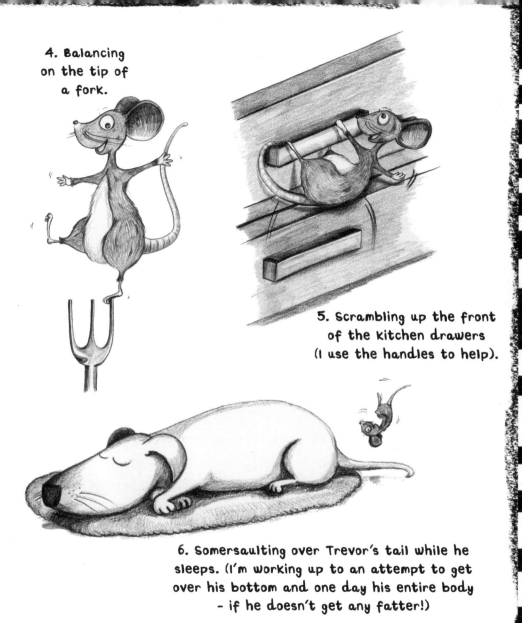

4. Balancing on the tip of a fork.

5. Scrambling up the front of the kitchen drawers (I use the handles to help).

6. Somersaulting over Trevor's tail while he sleeps. (I'm working up to an attempt to get over his bottom and one day his entire body - if he doesn't get any fatter!)

If I am feeling energetic – which I am tonight – I add in a special challenge. I have to choose four skills (four is my lucky number) and do them back to back. I call this the Stix Steeplechase.

Tonight, the order is:

KITCHEN DRAWERS > DRAINING RACK > BLIND SWING > TREVOR'S TAIL

I finish in record time, with a huge leap over Trevor's tail; it's the biggest jump I've done by far, and ... I nail it!

The landing is not quite as neat as I'd like, I land on my bottom then skid across the kitchen floor, but I've done it, and fast ... really fast.

I lie on the floor laughing quietly to myself. I wish someone had seen me. I bet it looked funny, me whizzing around like a lunatic.

At times like this, I wonder what it would be like to have a friend, someone to lie here and laugh with. Someone to play with other than a sleeping Trevor!

I look over at his plump, furry bum.

I'm not tired. I don't want to get back into the nest with Grandma yet. Perhaps this is the night, I whisper to myself ... the night I will do it. The night I will perform THE STIX SPECTACULAR and somersault over Trevor's bottom!

As I prepare myself, I realise that this is the most difficult and dangerous thing I have ever tried. I'm very excited and nervous all at once.

I perform another quick TREVOR WHISKER TICKLE. His nose doesn't even twitch; he's deep, deep asleep.

Next, I warm myself up, doing some special STIX STRETCHES.

5 star-jumps

4 sit-ups

3 roly-polys

1 press-up
(I hate these)

Once I've finished, I'm ready to go! To give myself the longest run-up possible, I walk to the far side of the kitchen. I take my usual four deep breaths (like I said, four is my lucky number) and begin my run.

I've just got up to maximum speed when I hear a sound that fills my body with terror.

The crrreeeak

of the kitchen

door opening!

MAXIMUS TROUBLE

My brain screams FREEZE – but I can't just stop. I'm going too fast! I plant my feet and find myself skidding towards Trevor. I dig my claws into the floor, cursing Grandma for making me chew them so short. I manage to stop just before I hit his water bowl.

Surely it can't be the mans? They never come down this late.

'A seen mouse is a dead mouse ...'

The words run through my head as I flatten myself against the floor. I can't see who has come in, but I CAN try to smell them. I take a good hard sniff. A bitter scent hits my nose. One I've not smelt before.

Out of the corner of my eye, I see something leap across the room towards me. I tuck myself into the tightest ball I can.

BOMPH. A sharp-clawed foot kicks me in the stomach, rolling me over. I open my eyes and find myself staring up at an enormous monster. It looks a lot like a mouse, only ten times bigger. And it's got yellow eyes and huge front teeth — they're as long as my arm!

'**What's wrong?**' snarls the monster. '**Never seen a rat before?**'

'N-no,' I stammer.

He laughs and, like an echo, I hear two other high-pitched laughs coming from just behind him. The laughter seems to be coming from the rat's body. I see his fur twitch and two fat, bald balls spring up on to his shoulder.

'I'm guessing from the look on your face you've never seen fleas before either,' sneers the rat. 'Well, I am Maximus, and this is Plague One ... and Plague Two.'

'He's small, but he looks juicy,' says Plague One.

'Yeah,' says Plague Two, gnashing its teeth, 'I can't wait to have a bite.'

'He's a littlun, all right,' laughs the rat, poking me with his toe. 'What are you? Some kind of miniature mouse?'

'Ha! Ha!' laughs Plague Two. 'You're big fat Maximus and he's skinny little Minimus. Geddit? Like Minnie Mouse.'

'I am NOT fat. Shut up!' says the rat angrily, swatting the fleas off his shoulder. 'Now listen, mouse,' he says, reaching a large paw down and wrapping it round my neck, 'we've come for the biscuits. Where are they?'

I glance across at Trevor. Now would be a **REALLY** good time for him to wake up ... but Trevor is so fast asleep, he's snoring. Maximus follows my gaze. 'Dogs are no threat to me,' he laughs. 'I beat them up for fun. Maximus by name, Maximus PAIN by nature!'

'Well, that's the first we've heard of it,' laughs Plague One. 'We've never seen you beat up a dog.'

'We did see you get chased by a cat, though,' sniggers Plague Two.

'Shut up! Shut UP!' snarls Maximus.

He yanks me to my feet.

'Now, I'm going to ask you one more time, mini mouse,' he growls, pressing his face unpleasantly close to mine. 'Where are the biscuits? Or I'll twist your teeny tiny head off.'

'I'm sorry, I can't.' I manage to squeak. 'It's Grandma's rule – we never touch the biscuits, not when they are in their packets.'

There is silence for a moment. Then the three of them burst out laughing.

'What kind of a dumb rule is that?' Maximus says, angrily spraying my face with spit. 'Don't tell me you're a pathetic mans fan?'

'What's a mans fan?' I choke.

'It means you dumbly believe it's a good idea to live in harmony with mans. It means you do all that silly hiding and not touching things nonsense. It means you are a MORON. Now tell me, moronic mans fan,' he says, tightening his grip on my neck, "WHERE. ARE. THE. BISCUITS?"

My brain screams, *Don't tell him, don't tell him.* But he's going to crush my windpipe. I'm starting to feel dizzy. Spots of light dance in front of my eyes.

I lift my arm and point weakly at the biscuit cupboard.

Maximus throws me to the floor and in three huge

bounds is at the cupboard. Using his long nose, he nudges open the door and with another leap, he's inside.

'Ginger Nuts, Hobnobs, Digestives!' he cries gleefully, slashing at the packets with his claws.

'Hooray!' cheer Plague One and Two. 'Perfect to sweeten your blood.'

'Which one shall I have?' Maximus says, staring at the mess he's made. 'Hmmmm, I think I'll have ... ALL OF THEM.'

He starts smashing biscuit after biscuit into his mouth. Crumbs fly everywhere. I watch in horror, powerless to stop him.

Then, as if things couldn't get any worse, my super-sensitive whiskers pick up a tremor. It's only the faintest movement, almost imperceptible, but there it is.

It's coming from upstairs. The mans are stirring in their bedroom.

'You've got to go,' I say, rushing towards the cupboard. 'You're making too much noise, you're waking up the mans. If they come in here and see us ... see this ... they'll ... they'll call Nuke-A-Pest!'

'Call Nuke-A-Pest?' laughs Maximus, spinning round to face me. A large chunk of Hobnob rolls off his belly and drops to the floor. 'Big deal. We rats live in the sewer beneath the building. Nuke-A-Pest never come down there.'

I pick up another tremor, this time stronger. I hear the sound of grumbling voices, then the creak of the bedroom door opening.

'**Please**,' I beg, '**please stop** ... they're coming.'

I look over at Trevor. His whiskers twitch – he's beginning to wake.

'Surely you've had enough,' I whisper, frantically trying to drag the wrappers to the back of the cupboard in the hope that I might hide them. I hear footsteps thundering down the stairs.

Trevor blinks a sleepy eye half open.

'**Dog!**' shouts Plague One. '**It's waking!**'

Without a word Maximus drops his Hobnob. In four huge bounds he makes it to the kitchen door and disappears.

Both Trevor's eyes fly open. He looks straight at me. I drop the wrapper.

'**Mouse!**' he barks, leaping excitedly to his feet. '**Mouse! Mouse! In the kitchen!**'

'**Trevor, what is wrong with you?**' shouts Schnookums. She's just outside the kitchen door now.

'It's the middle of the night ...'

I'm still trying to hide the biscuit crumbs and ripped-up wrappers, but it's too late! Schnookum's face appears round the door. My body freezes, I will myself to move, to run, but I can't, I'm paralysed by fear.

'Trevor, will you please—' she starts, but then suddenly she stops, and sees the mess of the biscuits and then what Trevor is barking at, and—

'ARRRRRRGGGGGGGH!!!!!!'

THE DEAD-MOUSE DECEPTION

Schnookums' ear-piercing scream shakes me into action. I run as fast as I can to the washing machine.

I tumble into the nest – and into Grandma.

'What's happening? What's going on?' she snaps crossly.

But when she sees how upset I am and I explain what happened,

her face softens. She pulls me into a big hug. 'There, there, Stix. You're safe now,' she says, pressing me into her warm fur.

Outside in the kitchen, Schnookums is still screaming. We hear the sound of MyLove's heavy steps thumping down the stairs. **'I'm warning you,'** we hear him say as he bursts into the kitchen, **'I've got a plant pot and I'm not afraid to use it ...'**

Schnookums stops screaming. 'It's OK, it was just a m–m–mouse,' she stammers.

'What? Where?' asks MyLove.

'I don't know. One minute it was right there, and the next it wasn't.'

I hold my breath. Grandma pulls me in tighter. Please don't let them find us ...

Then Mylove says, 'Darn it, well, that's that then ...'

And finally, the words I've been dreading all my life are uttered.

'We'll have to call Nuke-A-Pest in the morning.'

We listen to their footsteps disappear back up the stairs. Trevor goes quiet. Everything goes quiet, apart from my heart, which is pounding like a Maximus-sized fist in my chest.

'What are we going to do?' I ask, looking at Grandma. If only I'd listened to her rules. If only I hadn't gone out tonight.

'There's only one thing for it,' she says defiantly. **'There's only one way to save this situation ...'**

I wait nervously, knowing somehow that I'm not going to like the answer.

'I'm going to have to perform the Dead-Mouse Deception,' she says coolly.

'W-what's that?' I ask.

'When Nuke-A-Pest come, they'll tear the kitchen apart – they won't stop till they find this nest,' says Grandma, who is now pacing as she talks. 'Even if we're not here, it won't matter – they'll still lay poison and set traps. However, if they suspect there are no live specimens – if they come down in the morning and find me dead ... they won't. It's protocol.'

'D–dead?' I stammer. 'But—'

'I won't really be dead. I'm going to play dead.' She laughs. 'It's an old mouse's trick. I will drop my heart rate, make my body limp, and desensitise my eyes – just in case they go in for the poke. They like to do that sometimes, just to check I'm a proper goner.'

'But what will Nuke-A-Pest do with you?' I ask. 'Will they take you away?'

'No, no, they'll throw me in the rubbish bin or toss me on the compost heap. Don't you worry, my darling. I'll be back with you in no time,' she says with a wink, wrapping her arms round me and giving me an even bigger cuddle.

Grandma falls asleep in seconds. But I don't sleep a wink.

Nuke-A-Pest

Grandma wakes just before sunrise. I rub my eyes, pretending I've just woken up too.

'Now, whatever you do,' she says firmly, 'stay hidden, Stix, and don't come out until Nuke-A-Pest have gone.'

'B-b-but Grandma ...' I stutter.

'No buts,' she commands. 'I'll be back with you as soon as I can.'

And with that, she leaves our nest.

But I can't stay hidden – I can't just leave my brave, wonderful Grandma to face Nuke-A-Pest alone. I have to make sure she's OK. I wait a few seconds and then creep out of the nest after her.

I scramble up to the basket of washing that is always left on top of the washing machine. From the top I have a perfect view over the kitchen.

It doesn't take long for the mans to find her.

'**MOUSE!**' screams MyLove as he stumbles bleary-eyed into the kitchen. '**ARGGHHHHHHH! DEAD MOUSE!**'

If I wasn't so frightened,
I would say this was the
funniest thing I have ever
seen. How can such a huge
creature be scared of such a
small, supposedly dead one?

MyLove staggers back
and bangs into the
kitchen table.

'**AGHHHHHHH,**'
he cries, this time in pain.

Schnookums bursts in, holding a startled-looking Boo-Boo in
her arms. 'Is it back?' she gasps, clearly terrified. 'Where?'

'It's dead, don't worry,' says MyLove, pointing at Grandma.

'Not dead! Not dead!' barks Trevor, dancing around.
'Just pretending! Just pretending!'

'Shush, Trevor,' commands MyLove. 'Back on your rug.'

Trevor sulks back to his rug
and lies down. 'And there's
another in the washing
basket,' he growls.

40

'Why you not listen!'

'Well, at least Nuke-A-Pest won't have to tear the house up looking for it,' says Schnookums, striding over to the fridge. 'Let's call them in to get rid of it,' she says, ripping off their card and punching the number into her phone. 'Mouse,' she says. 'Dead. Yes, come immediately.'

'Mush deeeeaaa!' says Boo-Boo, mimicking her words. **'Meediatly.'**

Immediately means just that with Nuke-A-Pest. It's only minutes before there is a stern knock at the door. Schnookums plops Boo-Boo in her chair and rushes off down the hallway. MyLove cowers nervously in the corner, as far away from Grandma as he can get.

'Hello,' I hear a bright, cheery voice say. 'I'm Sheila, your Emergency Response Exterminator.'

41

A moment later, a round lady mans, with a face like a rosy apple, waddles in. She shakes MyLove's hand and strokes Boo-Boo's cheek. 'Aren't you a little cutie pie?' she coos.

As Schnookums points Sheila in the direction of Grandma, it's all I can do to stop myself running and jumping on top of her to protect her.

'**Well, well, well,**' Sheila says, bending over Grandma to take a closer look. 'It certainly looks dead, doesn't it?' She reaches into her back pocket and pulls out a pair of white rubber gloves.

'Tricky little blighters, though, mice,' she says, snapping them on. 'Always good to give them a close inspection, just to be surey-sure-sure-sure.'

She reaches down and clamps two fingers round Grandma's tail.

My stomach lurches – this is it. The moment of truth. Can Grandma fool them?

Sheila raises Grandma up to eye level and twirls her around, inspecting every inch of her body. My beautiful, wonderful grandma hangs limply, spinning in mid-air.

'Yup, it's deadingtons all right!' declares Sheila. 'Passed away an hour or two ago, I'd say. Probably gorged itself to death. Got any reason to suspect there might be more?'

I press myself down into a pair of MyLove's pants.

'Seen any droppings, any faecal matter?'

MyLove and Schnookums both shake their heads. 'Any other incidents like this recently?'

Again, they shake their heads in unison.

'Then I would say it's a rogue raid,' beams Sheila. 'For now, I advise we just monitor the situation. If you find a live one, however, or see any droppings, we'll escalate immediately to a Code Red and fumigate, not just the flat but the whole block — that'll get rid of all mice and, as a bonus, destroy any other vermin infestations you might have. We call it the "Double Whammy". It's my favourite of all the services we offer,' she adds gleefully.

I look at Grandma still playing perfectly dead. She really is so amazing! She's tricked the mans. She's saved us! I couldn't wish for a braver, more inspiring grandparent. I can't wait for this to be over so I can give her the biggest hug ever.

'So now all that's left to do is dispose of the little beastie,' smiles Sheila. 'If you'd show me to the toilet, please. New company policy dictates we flush small vermin.'

FLUSH?! WHAT??!

Grandma didn't say anything about this!

She's not a poo – she's a mouse. Grandma can't be flushed!

'No put mush in toilet,' says Boo-Boo. 'Mush is niye.'

'Mice are not nice, Boo-Boo, darling,' says Schnookums, 'especially not dead ones.'

She guides Sheila down the hallway to the bathroom. From the top of the washing basket I can still just see them. MyLove follows, keeping his distance.

Sheila holds Grandma in one hand and with the other opens the toilet lid. 'It won't get stuck in the U-Bend, will it?' asks MyLove.

'Don't you worry. A specimen this small'll flush like a

dream,' says Sheila matter-of-factly. 'If I'm not wrong, this block of flats discharges all its detritus into a septic tank. It'll be down there and composting with the rest of the waste before you can say "organic fertiliser".'

Grandma! Composting?! Organic fertiliser?!!

'NO! NO! NO!'

Unable to contain myself any longer, I cry out in horror. Luckily the mans are too far away to hear. But Boo-Boo does.

'Ickle mush, ickle mush,' she shouts, pointing at me with a pudgy finger. 'Mummy, mummy, ickle mush my nu fend. Me play ickle mush?'

'It's OK, sweetheart,' calls Schnookums. 'We haven't forgotten about you. We'll be back in a tick.'

I watch in horror as Sheila dangles Grandma over the toilet.

I pray Grandma misses, falls on the floor, runs back here to safety ... Please ...

'Bye-bye, Mrs Mouse,' says Sheila cheerily, releasing Grandma's tail. I watch her plummet like a mouse-shaped arrow straight into the toilet bowl.

45

PLOP! She hits the water.

Sheila leans forward and pulls the flush, then waits, peering into the toilet bowl.

'For a moment there I thought we had a floater –' she giggles – 'but it's gone. No need to double flush.'

My body goes numb. This can't be it. Tears tumble down my checks, plopping all around me, soaking a small wet patch on MyLove's pants. They fall and fall and won't stop as I realise –

Grandma's gone.

GONE. GONE. GONE.

My heart is suddenly as cold and heavy as a fridge.

It weighs me down.

I can't move. I sit paralysed watching Schnookums and MyLove making breakfast as if nothing has happened.

Finally, I find the strength to climb back down to our nest – I mean, my nest. I'm going to have to get used to saying that now it's just me, all on my own.

A tiny bit of me hopes Grandma is going to be there, that this was all some terrible nightmare. But of course she's not; there's just an empty space where she'd usually

47

be. I lie down and wrap my tail tightly round myself.

A tear tumbles down my cheek, then another, and another. My heart actually aches. Maybe Grandma was right ... Maybe hearts can break after all.

Eventually I cry myself to sleep.

ALONE

When I wake it's dark.

I drag myself out of the nest, though I'm not really sure why. It's not like I want to eat — I don't think I'll ever feel hungry again.

Trevor is snoring loudly in his basket.

I look out from my hiding place. How will I ever get used to not having Grandma with me? She's always been there, at my side, protecting me, telling me what to do.

I feel a sob rise up in my throat. I look over at Trevor. Would it be so bad if I let it out? If it woke him? Maybe then Sheila would come and flush me as well. At least, in a strange, dead sort of way, I would be with Grandma.

I crawl
back into
my nest again
and try to go
back to sleep.

A BAT
(NOT A RAT)

When I wake the next time, I've no idea how long I've slept. It's dark and my stomach is rumbling, so I guess it must have been a while.

I consider not leaving the nest at all. I wonder what would happen if I just lay here for ever? It's not like anyone is going to come looking for me. But my stomach growls again and I change my mind and creep out.

When I get into the kitchen, something is missing. It takes me a moment to work out what. It's Trevor. His rug is there but he's gone. Then I spot a note on the blackboard.

Strangely, I feel relieved knowing he'll be back. He's the only company I've got now – I don't care that he's always asleep.

The mans had macaroni for supper. I find a large
chunk next to the sink. I love macaroni — usually I'd
gobble it up, but my appetite has gone. All I manage is a
tiny nibble.

The kitchen is lighter than usual. The big ball
of light in the sky is
large and full tonight,
and there are little
twinkles all around it.
I climb up on to the
kitchen countertop
and press my nose up
against the window
to get a better look
at it. I suddenly feel
very small, and very
alone.

I wonder what my
life will be like now
Grandma's gone. Will
I ever talk to anyone

again? Will I eat every meal on my own? Will I spend every evening all by myself?

'Please ...' I say, gazing up at the big ball of light, 'give me a sign ... give me some hope that I won't be lonely for ever.'

I wait, staring into the darkness, looking for something, anything ... a flicker, a movement, a twinkle to shine a little brighter.

But I see nothing, nothing different.

My heart sinks.

I let out a long, sad sigh.

And that's when –

THWACK.

Something black hits the window and attaches itself to the glass.

I leap backwards in terror and, finding nothing to hide behind, flatten myself on to the countertop.

'Hey there! Oh, hey! Stop. Please don't run away. I'm a bat. I won't harm you,' it calls out.

'Did you say, "r–r–rat"?' I stammer.

'Rat?? Heehahahaha! I'm not a RAT! I'm a BAT! I am way different. For a start I've got these.'

I look up. The creature is jet black. Its body is small and furry like mine, only, unlike me, on each side of it are two huge flappy things.

'They're wings,' says the bat, its face breaking into a broad grin. 'Wings ... you know ... for flying.'

Flying! I want to say, 'WOW! Amazing! Really? Flying? I wish I could do that!' But I'm so scared that all I can manage is a tiny squeak.

'**I'm Batz**,' says the strange creature, pressing its nose against the window, 'and, yeah, I know that's kind of like a boy's name and I'm a girl, but whatever, so what, who cares? Not me! Hey, you're that mouse, aren't you? One of the secret mice. The ones no one in Peewit Mansions ever sees. This is so exciting. I mean, I've always wondered if you're really real and now here you are, and here I am. This is just totally awesome,' she says, finally pausing for breath.

'It ... I–I ...' I stutter, but I don't know what to say. I had no idea that anyone apart from us lived in the building, let alone that they knew about ME.

'**Heehahahahaha!**' she laughs. 'You're so funny. You don't even know what you are! You're kind of famous, you know? Famous for being invisible. I mean, we ALL hide from the mans, but you hide from pests too! My third cousin says I'm dumb for even believing you exist. But I knew, I KNEW if I waited long enough I'd spot you – and I have – and when I tell him, he's going to be SO bummed. Heehahahaha!'

I wonder if all bats talk so much and have such a strange laugh?

'In fact,' Batz continues, 'it's so exciting that we HAVE to have this conversation face to face!'

And with that, she detaches herself and disappears into the dark. I stand rooted to the spot. What does she mean face to face? How is she going to get through the glass? Break it?

I hear a swoosh and spin round to find her swooping across the kitchen towards me. She lands silently on the plate rack, hanging herself upside down.

'**How did you ...?**' I gasp.

'Up the roof, down the chimney, out of the fireplace, across the living room, into the kitchen!' she says, dusting some soot from her fur. 'So, secret mouse, what's your name?'

'**Er, I'm Stix,**' I say.

'Well, Stix,' she grins, showing off two lines of neat, pointy teeth, 'it's so good to finally meet you. Is it true you're home-schooled?'

'Home what?' I ask.

'You know, taught at home. My mum told me you were. Your grandma teaches you. You live with her, right?'

I think about telling her the awful truth – that Grandma's gone, that I'm all alone – but when I try, I get a lump in my throat, so I just nod.

'What's it like not going to school? Is it weird? I bet it is.'

'What's school?' I ask, confused. Grandma never taught me that word.

'Heehahahaha! You are sooooo funny!' Batz laughs. 'That's a good one. What's school! Dry sense of humour, I like it.'

I look at my feet, feeling rather embarrassed. 'I honestly don't know what you're talking about,' I say quietly.

'Oh,' she says, looking surprised. 'Right. So you have no idea about P.E.S.T.S. – **The Peewit Educatorium for Seriously Terrible Scoundrels.** The school in the basement?'

I shake my head.

'Wow,' she says, crossing her eyes, 'mind-bending!'

I can't help but laugh, she looks so funny, and she does

it again. Then she smiles at me. 'You know what, I like you. You're cool. You should come to school, find out what it's all about for yourself. I mean, yeah, you've missed most of the year. But who cares! I'm sure you'd catch up. It'll be fun! Go on ...' She stops, noticing the clock on the oven.

'Yikes! Is that the time? Class starts at midnight. That's in five minutes! I'm gonna be late. Gotta go!'

And with that, she disappears through the kitchen door and is gone.

AM I MAD?

Did that really just happen? Did I really just have a conversation with a bat who said we should be friends and invited me to a secret school in the basement?

I can't believe Grandma never told me about it. For a moment I feel cross, but then the sadness overwhelms me. She was only trying to keep me safe. It's hard for a mouse to stay alive.

Thinking about Grandma makes me want to go back to our nest, curl up in a ball and cry. But then it suddenly it hits me. If I stay here, in Flat 3, then this is what my life will be: crawling out of my nest to eat and then crawling back into it again. Me, all alone, night after night, with only the occasional somersault over a sleeping dog's bottom to entertain me. But if I go with Batz ...

I look out across the hallway. There it is: The Frontier Door. The edge of my world. The line that divides me from The Beyond, divides me from this secret place, somewhere maybe I would have a friend.

Would it really be so bad if I slipped underneath the door? Would it be so terrible? Surely Grandma wouldn't want me to stay here all alone?

I take a step forward. Then another, and before I know it, I am leaping off the kitchen countertop and running down the hallway as fast as I can. I can't stop, I mustn't stop. I have to keep going, otherwise I might give in to the petrified voice in my head that is screaming,

'DON'T DO THIS, STIX. YOU'RE MAD!!!!!'

And suddenly here I am, standing at the foot of The Frontier door, shaking like one of Boo-Boo's strawberry jellies. I feel excited and scared all at once.

I poke my nose through the gap between the floor and the door and I take my first ever sniff of The Beyond. It smells of carpet and a hint of wood polish. Nothing to be afraid of – yet.

I flatten my body against the floor, and slowly, carefully slide myself through the gap ... I do one more check, my nose pokes out from under the door and, a moment later, my body wriggles out into ...

THE BEYOND

This is it.

This is The Beyond.

And it's ...

... VAST.

It stretches out in front of me, it stretches out above me.

I stand up on my hind legs, sniffing deeply, trying to take it all in. The air is cool and feels somehow heavier — thick with new smells.

I'm at one end of an enormous hallway. The floor is covered in green carpet, old and worn. The walls are so tall I can barely see the ceiling.

I suddenly feel extremely small and very vulnerable.

I fight the urge to crawl back under the door to the safety of Flat 3.

Grandma taught me about up and down, ceilings and floors, attics and basements, so I know that the basement will be at the very bottom of the building. I look to my left – at the end of the corridor is a huge window. I look to my right – there's a staircase, with steps leading down. I know what I have to do.

The stairs are huge and steep and there are so many, but I'm not going to let fear stop me now.

I race down them, taking each one in a single gigantic bound, getting faster and faster as I go, all the way down until, in one huge last leap, I make it to the bottom. I stand, panting for a moment, my limbs trembling. If it wasn't so terrifying, I'd say it was the most fun I've ever had.

I look around as I catch my breath. I'm in another corridor, like the one upstairs, but this time there are no more stairs, only a great big door, even bigger than The Frontier Door, and my senses are telling me it leads out rather than down.

What now? I scurry over to the wall and press myself

tight up against it. I put my ears on red alert — pricking them as high as they will go. I fan my whiskers and place my nose on CSM (constant Sniff Mode). Then I hold myself still, waiting, hoping for a sign to show me the way.

For a moment there is nothing but silence, then I feel a faint twinge in my left whisker, a vibration. I'm picking up a sound. But not the sound of mans — a new sound.

I creep further along the wall. The tingle spreads to both

whiskers. I stop, and this time I smell something new too, a faint mustiness. Didn't Grandma say that basements were full of old stuff?

I look around, trying to work out where the sound and the smell are coming from, and that's when I notice, just ahead of me, set low into the wall — a metal grille.

Through the grille comes the faint sound of laughter. 'Heehahahahaha!'

Batz! This must be it, the way down to the basement.

Carefully I wiggle myself into the gap between two of the grille's metal slats. On the other side it's almost completely dark. But that's not a problem for

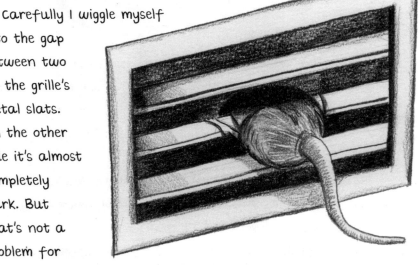

me. I use my whiskers to feel my way. First, I feel brick, and then something cold ... and slippery and ... suddenly the floor beneath me is sloping steeply down! I start to slide. I try to reverse back, but my front feet can't get a grip. I face-plant forward and, before I know it, find myself skidding head first down a narrow metal tube. I let out a panicked squeal as, seconds later, I'm out of the tube and flying through the air, and then ...

BOMPH. To my relief I land on something soft – and very, very dusty. A cushion perhaps. I can hardly breathe or see from all the dust.

'**ATCH-OOO!**' I sneeze loudly.

As the dust begins to clear, I peer out into the gloom. I can see a huge rickety old wardrobe, one door missing and the other hanging on by a hinge. And inside the wardrobe I can just make out ... a set of eyes, and then another, and another, and another, and then ...

'**Stix!**' I hear a voice cry. I look up to see another set of eyes, high above the others, apparently hanging upside down. It's Batz, waving manically.

And behind Batz, across the back of the wardrobe,

sprayed large in luminous paint, are the letters:

I've found it!

P.E.S.T.S.

As my eyes adjust to the gloom, I take in a curious collection of creatures inside the wardrobe. Most are sat on the floor at one end – or hanging from a clothes rail in Batz's case. At the other end, perched on top of an old shoebox, is a large, plump pigeon.

'Darlinks,' coos the pigeon, pronouncing the word very strangely, 'we appear to have a new pupil. Either that or we have the smallest attacking army I have ever seen.'

'Er, n–new pupil,' I stammer.

'Well, you're not going to learn very much sitting up there,' tuts the pigeon.

I scrabble to my feet and look down. I appear to be

standing on a large, moth-eaten cushion, perched on a chair. I guess that I'm at least 50 mouse heights above the ground.

Using my well-practised 'chair-leg sliding skills', I slither down to the floor and hurry across to the wardrobe. From the chair the wardrobe looked big, but from down here, on the floor, it looks **GIGANTIC.** It towers above me. I'm just wondering how in the name of mature Cheddar I'm going to get myself up and into it, when I notice a cobweb-covered lamp. It's fallen against the wardrobe, making the perfect ramp.

I scramble up it as fast as I can, tumble off the end and find myself at the foot of the shoebox.

'Well, well, well,' coos the pigeon, peering down at me intently. I notice that one of her eyes is much bigger than the other. **'If I'm not mistaken, it's Hazel's grandson.'**

I blink. How does she know my grandma's name? How does she know who I am?

'Well, mouse, darlink,' she says with a warm smile, 'I would be very happy to have you in my class. In fact, I would go as far as to say I am excited. If you are half the student

your parents were, then you'll no doubt flourish here.'

'My p–parents? But how d—'

From somewhere behind, I'm interrupted by a cruel laugh.

'Well, look who it is ...'

I hear him and smell him before I see him.

His unmistakable bitter scent makes every muscle in my body tense. I look down and sure enough there he is, scampering up the lamp – **Maximus**. I hear Plagues One and Two snigger from his fur. My teeth clench, my paws ball into fists. I try to put thoughts of the last time we met, the last night I spent with my grandma, out of my mind as I feel my body temperature rise.

'Maximus!' tuts the pigeon. 'That's enough from you. You're late. That's one Golden Point deducted. Now sit down and be quiet or I'll take off another.'

She turns round and behind her I notice a huge blackboard. On it is written in big letters: PEST OF THE YEAR – LEADERBOARD. Below that is a list of everyone's names and next to them a number.

Maximus: 92, Dug: 52, Blue: 50, Underlay: 47, Batz: 46 and Webbo: 42.

She rubs off Maximus's score and replaces it with a 91.

While her back is turned, Maximus shoves past me and takes a seat at the back of the wardrobe. 'Out of my way, mans fan,' he mutters.

'Now, class,' says the pigeon turning to face us, 'as we

Pest of The Year

Maximus 91
Dug   52
Blue   50
Underlay 47
Batz   46
Webbo 42

have a new pupil, I suggest we have a sharing assembly. It's the perfect way for him to meet his fellow classmates,' she adds, smiling at me. 'To give you an idea of how this works, I shall offer a quick demonstration.'

She ushers me to sit with the rest of the class. I take my place next to a furry creature with the biggest paws I have ever seen. He smiles kindly, though his eyes are so tiny I am surprised he can even see me.

The pigeon clears her throat and declares loudly, 'My name is Dr Krapotkin. I have a double degree in Disorder and Insubordination and a PhD in Anarchy.' As she says this, she puffs up the feathers on her chest to reveal a symbol – the letter 'A' ringed by a circle.

'I was hatched in Hell, by which I mean that manky old shopping centre on the other side of town. As a chick I was poked in the eye by an over-eager mans child, which is why I have this' – she swivels her head round to show off her very small eye – 'and, as you can also see, I have one wing that is better groomed than the other. This is because, like all good anarchists, I favour my left. The left wing is always preferable to the right, darlinks, always. Now,' she says, turning to face us, 'enough about me. Let's hear all about you, you little hell-raisers!'

One at a time, everyone else has their go.

There is:

A very large bluebottle called Blue, who says his passion is being sick on things and buzzing around really loudly.

A carpet beetle called Underlay, who speaks so fast I can hardly understand what she says - I just about make out the words 'shagpile' and 'tasty'. In her claws she clutches a tiny piece of worn woolly material she calls her 'comfort carpet'.

A shy mole called
Dug - the one with
the huge paws and
small eyes - who
claims to be able
to destroy a lawn
in just one night.

A large brown spider called
Webbo who proudly says
he's great at 'well-scary
web spinning' and that the
secret to his success is his
'awesome silk-producing
bum'.

Then, of course, there is **Batz**. She says she lives in the roof with her parents and fifty-two aunts, uncles, nieces, nephews, great-aunts, great-uncles and various grandparents. She says she is an expert in making roof tiles shake, and that her favourite thing is telling

jokes. She then tells us all her favourite joke –
'What's brown and sticky?

Sticks ... like Stix ... geddit?'

I can't help but laugh – but no one else does. Batz turns and flashes me a big grin.

Maximus goes last. He stands up tall and declares, 'I am Maximus Raticus the 162nd. I come from a long line of highly intelligent, over-achieving rats. My interests are inflicting pain and being the best – both of which I do **VERY** well.'

Plagues One and Two clap from somewhere in his fur.

'Oh, and these are my fleas,' he says. 'Together, their ancestors and mine were personally responsible for the bubonic plague, which wiped out twenty-five million mans. We're, like, the dream team!'

Dr Krapotkin claps kindly after every speech. I had been kind of hoping that she would forget about me, but of course she doesn't.

'Now, mouse, darlink,' she smiles, 'it is your turn. Please do tell us a little about yourself.'

Everyone looks at me. Batz smiles encouragingly. Maximus flashes me a nasty, toothy grin.

My heart starts to pound. It feels like it's suddenly grown as big as my body, like I'm made of heartbeat. I have never had to talk like this, in front of other creatures, before. I open my mouth to speak, but it feels as dry as dust.

'Well ... I ... er, I ... um ...' I manage to stammer, then I freeze. This is awful. My mind has gone completely blank, like I don't know a single thing about myself.

'Why don't you start by telling us your name, darlink,' says Dr Krapotkin kindly.

'I'm ... I'm Stix,' I say. 'I'm a mouse.'

'Obviously,' I hear Maximus mutter, and Plagues One and Two titter in unison.

Dr Krapotkin fixes him with her small eye. **'Do you want to lose another point?'** she says. Maximus scowls, but shuts up at least.

'And ...' I continue, doing my best to ignore him, trying to think of something to say about myself that's interesting, 'and I love practising my skills and climbing stuff and jumping over things, like, er ... Trevor ... the, er ... dog.' I feel myself blush under my fur. I stare at the floor, wishing it would swallow me up.

'Excellent! Well done, Stix,' says Dr Krapotkin, applauding my effort. 'I can tell that wasn't easy for you. For being so brave I am going to award you 40 Golden Points.'

'What? No way!' blurts Maximus. 'That's loads. You can't—'

'And given this is your third interruption today,' says Dr Krapotkin, swivelling her neck almost all the way round to face him, 'I am also going to deduct ten from you, Maximus. There,' she says, adding my name to the leaderboard and giving me a 40, then adjusting Maximus down to an 81! 'All looking a bit more evened out now, aren't we, darlinks? And we still have a few challenges left to come — not to mention the big, final award from our visiting professor, of course! So even though Stix started a bit late, he still has some chance of catching you all up and being named PEST OF THE YEAR.'

When Dr Krapotkin isn't looking, Maximus leans menacingly towards me and mouths: **'The award is MINE.'**

He grins, his top lip curling up to reveal the full length of his two massive front teeth.

The ones that gnawed the biscuits.

The ones that got Grandma flushed down the loo.

And, all of a sudden, I know what I have to do. Something that will cause him pain — like the pain he's caused me. Because I can see now what he wants more than anything.

I must take his dream away from him, just as he took Grandma from me.

I must win.

Pest of The Year

Maximus 81
Dug   52
Blue   50
Underlay 47
Batz   46
Stix   40
Webbo   42

RULES 'N' STUFF

'Now, darlinks,' says Dr
Krapotkin, 'it is very important
that, before we continue, Stix
knows and understands the five
rules of P.E.S.T.S. Who would like
to tell him what they are?'

Maximus is about to shout them
out, but at the same time Dug's
enormous paw flies up in the air.
'Me, Miss, me!' he begs.

Dr Krapotkin nods, giving Maximus a warning look, and Dug proceeds to tell me that:

1. **A good pest is heard but never seen.**
2. **A good pest is always one step ahead.**
3. **A good pest bothers but never harms.**
4. **A good pest has fun but covers its tracks.**
5. **A good pest never goes too far.**

'Rule 5, darlink, is the most important of all,' says Dr Krapotkin. 'Being a pest is about having fun. It's about anarchy — being a REBEL. But it's not about doing terrible damage, or hurting the mans. Yes, the mans would squish us, trap us, do terrible things to us ... but that doesn't mean we wish the same on them. That would be foolish — mans are an important source of food and shelter. If there were no mans, we would lose all that. And if we go too far, or they realise we are here, they call Nuke-A-Pest, no questions asked. However, that is not to say that we accept the mans as our masters. We most definitely do NOT. Mans bother us and make our lives difficult, and it is our duty to pay them back. So we have FUN. We do a little bothering. We cause a little trouble. But we **NEVER go**

too far. Do you understand, Stix, darlin—'

But before I get the chance to reply, the basement is suddenly filled with a deafening rattling noise, followed by the thunderous sound of rushing water. My senses tell me it is coming from above.

'**Ahh, the poop pipe,**' shouts Dr Krapotkin, nervously

Poop pipe

shuffling further into the wardrobe. She points up at a large black pipe that travels the length of the basement, hanging just below the height of the ceiling. 'Mans take a number two and – *whoosh* – down it comes, across the ceiling on its way to the poop tank. Now, class, if you are ever down here and you hear it, make sure you are in the safety of the wardrobe. If that inspection cap comes loose again,' she says, pointing her wing at a large, round lump in the middle of the pipe, 'you will be taking a disgusting "poo shower" like I did last year. Pigeons should be pooping on mans, not the other way round! I was very lucky it wasn't solid,' she says gravely. **'A solid poop, dropping from that height, could have knocked my head off.'**

I can tell everyone finds this very funny and are struggling to hide it.

'Now, darlinks,' she continues, patting down her ruffled feathers as the poo pipe gives one last rattle and falls silent, 'it is time for your practical assessment. Tonight you are going to give me a demonstration of your most fantastic bothering skills. I will be awarding you marks for both effort and energy. A maximum of ten for each. So, who would like to go first?'

Maximus rubs his paws gleefully.

I smile through gritted teeth, trying to pretend I am not totally, utterly petrified. Because I can't fail, I must not fail.

SKILLS

'To give you a clear idea of what you will have to do to get the perfect twenty,' says Dr Krapotkin, 'I shall give you a quick demonstration. Imagine those cardboard boxes over there are cars.'

She takes a deep breath and then launches herself off her shoebox, gliding silently towards the boxes. 'This is a special trick we pigeons call "CAR-nage ..." Get it? Imagine this box is a nice shiny car, a BMW ideally, and this one an Audi. Maybe a Range Rover here, something flashy and expensive. Now watch carefully, darlinks. I fly over these automobiles ... I wait until the optimum moment, then I open my bottom and – **"Ta-daaaaa!"** In a split second the boxes are completely covered in runny white poo. 'Total turd-splurge. Thanks to the highly acidic content of my do-do, there is no doubt these cars would be needing a new paint job!'

We give her a round of applause as she returns to her shoebox. I can't help but wonder what she ate for breakfast.

'Now, darlinks,' she says, 'it's your turn. Knock me out!'

Blue buzzes around our heads so fast he's just a blur. 'Szzwat me! Szzwat me' he calls out, but he's way too fast. The noise of his buzzing fills the wardrobe. After a while, Dr Krapotkin stops him, complaining he's giving her a headache. This, she clarifies, is a positive thing. **He gets 15.**

'Watchmeeasilychewthisantiquerugintwo,' gabbles Underlay gleefully as she chews through an old rug. She says it tastes like a precious heirloom. **She gets 15 too.**

Dug demonstrates how fast he can dig by burrowing his way through a huge box of old

clothes. He makes it from one side to the other in less than two seconds. He says if this was a manicured lawn, he'd have destroyed it.

He gets 16.

Webbo spins a very intricate web between two rusty candlesticks. He then positions his large body in the middle of the web, and spreads out his long, hairy legs. He tells us to imagine the candlesticks are on a posh dining table, and that the mans have just sat down for dinner. He says they would no doubt 'pee their panties'. Dr Krapotkin points out that being seen would probably mean being squished and **gives him a 10.**

Batz shows us how she scares the mans by flying into their windows and then twitching around on the floor like she's been seriously injured. She demonstrates on the mirror that hangs on the inside of the wardrobe door. Her performance is so convincing that I believe for a moment that she really has hurt herself. Until she starts laughing her head off ... She loses points for not taking the test seriously – which strangely seems to please her, and make her laugh even more.

She gets 9.

Then it's Maximus's turn. He bounds over to a tangle of old electrical cables that spills out from a black bin liner. Swiftly, one at a time, he gnaws through them, his huge front teeth chomping up and down like a pair of vicious scissors. He makes light work of even the fattest cable.

'Do it! chew it! Do it! chew it!' chant Plagues One and Two from somewhere on his body.

In no time at all Maximus has chewed through the lot. He bounds proudly back to the wardrobe.

'**Excellent work!**' claps Dr Krapotkin. '**A perfect 20.** Great style and execution.'

'**Beat that, mouse,**' he snarls in my ear as he shoves past me, stamping down hard on my left back paw.

'**Maximus!**' snaps Dr Krapotkin. '**I saw that!**'

'It was an accident!' he replies innocently.

But a voice from above me shouts, 'It wasn't an accident, Miss, he did it on purpose. I saw him do it, and he said something horrible too. I heard everything!'

It's Batz. She swoops down and stands beside me in support. I smile across at her. I don't think I've ever been more grateful to anyone in my life.

'Hmmm,' says Dr Krapotkin, looking at Maximus 'in that case, darlink, I am afraid I will be taking away all your marks for this exercise.'

'What!' he cries. **'No way! No way! That's not fair! I always get top marks.'**

'Well, not today,' Dr Krapotkin says coldly.

Maximus storms to the back of the wardrobe, sitting down with a loud, angry huff.

'Now, Stix, are you OK to continue?' asks Dr Krapotkin.

This is it, my chance to catch up.

'Yes,' I answer as enthusiastically as I can, but I have no idea what I am going to do. I hoped when it came to my turn that something would miraculously pop into my head. But that hasn't happened. I'm just not used to being bad. Everything Grandma ever taught me was about staying hidden, staying safe, Keeping It Tidy ...

Think! Think! Think!

I quickly go through Grandma's rules in my head — all the things she told me never to do. I settle on one in particular ... the second rule of Keeping it Tidy ...

Never chew holes in cardboard or plastic containers ...

OK, I think. I can do this. It's just ...

I hear a nasty chorus of cackles. It's Maximus and the Plagues. 'I don't think he's got what it takes, Miss,' giggles Maximus. 'He's too small and weak. You should send him home to his grandma, Miss.'

If Dr Krapotkin replies, I don't hear. My body is suddenly filled with a furious rage, my head with the THUD! THUD! THUD! of pumping blood. How dare he say those words! I can't go home to my grandma! My grandma is gone — because of HIM!!!

I rear up on to my back legs, my muscles surging with a fierce, powerful energy, a kind I have never felt before.

But instead of launching myself at Maximus, I launch myself off the edge of the wardrobe, towards a tatty cardboard box. I'm going to destroy it. I use everything I've got — my teeth, my jaws, my paws ...

Slash! Slash! Slash! go my claws.

Gnash! Gnash! Gnash! go my teeth.

Whump! Whump! Whump! goes my tail.

I can't see anything but the blur of my body moving beneath me.

I keep on and on, until the cardboard is shredded so small I can't shred any more. I stagger backwards and look down at what I've done. Where a few seconds ago there was a box, there is now just a pile of chewed-up, ripped-up card. I rub my eyes and blink. Did I really just do this?

Then from somewhere above me, I hear clapping. I look up and see everyone else smiling down at me. Batz is making loops-the-loops in the air.

'You totes smashed it, dude!' cries Webbo, clapping wildly.

Dug and Blue both race over to congratulate me.

'**Zzzzzuperdouper,**' buzzes Blue excitedly, circling my head, making me dizzy.

Dr Krapotkin claps her wings. Everyone looks so happy.

Well, everyone but Maximus. He looks angry, very angry.

'Very impressive indeed, darlink,' smiles Dr Krapotkin. 'For such a small thing, you have created an incredibly big mess. And in such a short space of time. For that I am going to award you 19 points. I am afraid I have to take off one mark for hesitation, but apart from that, it was an exemplary performance. Now, that's quite enough excitement for one night. Off to bed, everyone!'

Batz beams down at me. 'Well done, Stix!' she mouths before swooping off across the basement. 'See ya tomorrow!' I watch as she

Pest of The Year

Maximus	81
Dug	68
Blue	65
Underlay	62
Batz	55
Stix	59
Webbo	52

wiggles herself out through a small window at the very top of the wall.

A moment later, everyone else has gone too. For a moment the loneliness hits me again, as well as the realisation that I don't know how to get home. I can't climb back up the slippery pipe — it's too steep. But I don't want to go home anyway. It will bring back too many horrible memories.

I spot an old sofa by the wall next to the wardrobe. It looks like a good place to sleep. I climb up and tuck myself behind one of its musty cushions. It's weird being on my own again, but I think back to Batz sticking up for me, swooping down to stand by my side, cheering me on, and although I'm exhausted and totally drained,

100

I feel happy. For the first time in my life **I have a friend**. A real friend. I miss my grandma with every bone in my body, but at least I'm not alone any more.

THE BLAME GAME

'OK, my darlinks, it is time for class! Gather round!'

For a moment I have no idea where I am. Then it all comes back to me – Batz at my window, P.E.S.T.S., sleeping down the back of the sofa. With a start I realise that's still where I am. I must have overslept.

I creep down the side of the sofa and run over to the wardrobe, up the lamp, taking my seat quietly next to Dug. I look up and catch Batz's eyes, and she waves down at me.

'So, class, yesterday we worked on some of our best bothering skills. Tonight we are going to go one step further and look at ways we can make the mans doubt who is to blame for the botherings. I call this module "The Blame Game".'

Dr Krapotkin turns to the blackboard and proceeds to draw a mans' shoe. She adds a large hole in its toe.

'Would anyone like to suggest what has happened here?' she asks.

'A big, clever rat chewed it,' says Maximus proudly.

'**Wrong!**' says Dr Krapotkin brightly. 'And how about this ...'

She starts drawing again. This time she draws what she calls a 'garden'. In the middle of it is a big mound of earth.

Dug immediately jumps up. 'A mole! Miss, a mole did it!'

'**Wrong again!**' says Dr Krapotkin. 'If a mans thinks that a rat has chewed a hole in this shoe, or a mole has dug a hole in this lawn, then we are in big trouble. Remember we are trying to shift blame away from ourselves. So, would anyone like to suggest another creature who might have chewed or dug these holes?'

A loud buzzing sound fills the wardrobe. It's Blue.

'Dogzzzzzzzz didt,' he says, hovering up above us so he can be seen.

'Very good, Blue! A point for you.' Dr Krapotkin smiles. 'We make it look like a dog did it. There are two easy ways we can do this.'

On the board she writes: PLANT SOME EVIDENCE.

'One. We could take a small piece of the shoe we have destroyed and place it in the dog's bed. Or, we could take a little soil and carefully, while the dog is sleeping, rub it on its paws. Bingo! The mans will have a wrecked shoe, or a trashed lawn, and it will be Rover who will be getting all the blame. Ha! Ha! Ha!'

She wipes the board clean with a sweep of her wing. 'If we are clever, we might even make the mans take the blame for our botherings. Let's say Maximus here has had a little nibble on this biscuit.' She draws a biscuit with some teeth marks in it.

Memories of Maximus chomping his way through the biscuit cupboard come flashing back, but I push them away and try to concentrate.

'What he must now do is bite larger, mans-sized teeth

marks into it.'

She draws larger teeth marks around the smaller ones.

'This way, when the mans finds the biscuit, it will look like another mans has been eating it. Perhaps a child, a wife, a husband, a grandparent ...

'And if we take this one step further ... perhaps we can leave the mans with no idea who's to blame at all. "What's making that terrible buzzing?" they will wonder.' She smiles at Blue, who gives a little excited buzz. 'Or "What is tickling my foot?".' Webbo chuckles knowingly. 'Does this all make sense, darlinks?'

We all nod.

'Good, because tonight's homework is to put all this into practice. I want you to go and do something really bothersome, making sure the mans have no idea who is really to blame. I will be awarding Golden Points for both ingenuity and cunning. And remember, the flies-on-the-walls will be watching you and then reporting back to me. So make it good, darlinks. **Make it exemplary.**'

TARQUIN THE DUDE

Apparently there are four flats in Peewit Mansions, each with different mans living in it.

Dr Krapotkin splits us up as follows:

Blue and Underlay, Flat 1.

Maximus and the Plagues, Flat 2.

Webbo, Flat 3.

Batz and me, Flat 4. (Whoop! My lucky number!)

Dug, of course, gets the garden.

'Hey, partner,' says Batz, swooping down, 'gimme five!'

'Give you what?' I ask.

'Heehahahee! You really are too funny,' she laughs. 'Come on, let's go. I'll race you there.'

'Hold up!' I call after her. She turns back, waiting for me to say something. I lower my voice in embarrassment. 'Wait ... I ... I don't know how to get to Flat 4.'

'Whaaaat?' she says, looping back. 'Are you seriously telling me you don't know about the **hidden highways?**'

I shake my head.

'Geez, I think you just blew my mind for the second time! Come on,' she says, swooping off again, 'follow me. I'll show you the entrance.'

I follow her to a patch of crumbling wall on the other side of the basement.

'**Ta-da!**' she says gleefully, pointing at four small holes. 'Each one leads to a different highway, and each highway leads to a different flat. They're in order, so the one on the far right leads to Flat 4. Obvs I don't need to use them. I use windows and vents and chimneys – far easier. See you at the top!'

I wiggle into the fourth hole and find myself in a tunnel gnawed out of foam.

The tunnel climbs steeply upwards. The foam is spongy and yet firm. My claws sink into it, making it easy for me to grip. I begin to climb. After a few minutes, I reach a grey plastic pipe cutting across the foam tunnel. The foam all around it had been chewed away so I can climb along on top of it. In the distance, at the end of the pipe, I can see a tiny pinprick of light. This must be the way out!

Eventually I find myself at the end of the tunnel. I poke my nose out and take a long deep sniff. I smell bleach, shampoo and soap. The tunnel has led me to a bathroom.

I wiggle out and find myself staring at a white, shiny wall. I scramble up it and then realise – I am on top of a toilet. As I look down, memories of Grandma's flushing come rushing back.

Don't think about it, I tell myself, squeezing my eyes tight shut, trying to block out the thought.

'**Hey! What's up, Stix?**' It's Batz. She's hanging from the towel rail. 'What's with the long face?'

'It's, just, well, er, toilets ...' I say, a knot of sadness twisting in my stomach.

She looks confused.

I take a deep breath. 'My grandma died in a toilet. She

got ... flushed away. By Nuke-A-Pest.'

'What? But ... but you said you lived with her. I don't understand.' Batz looks even more confused.

'I know, I know. I didn't mean to lie, it's just that I didn't want to tell the truth either.' I pause and sigh. 'I did live with her. But I don't any more. Because ...' And then the whole story comes flooding out. The words tumble from my mouth, about Maximus and the biscuits and the mess and the mans waking up and Nuke-A-Pest and Grandma saving me by doing the Dead-Mouse Deception but then getting flushed down the loo.

When I'm finished, I pause for breath. I notice my heart feels lighter, like talking about what happened has made it feel somehow just a tiny bit better.

'That bone-head, numb-skull, pea-brained, selfish, mega-moron, bag-of-badbones rat!' shrieks Batz.

I glance around nervously, checking no one has heard.

'We need to get him back! And you know the best way to do it?' Says Batz.

'Stop him winning Pest of the Year,' I say nervously, hoping that's what she's thinking too.

'**Exactamundo** ... and you need to win!'

'But what about you? Don't you want to win?' I ask nervously, as it suddenly dawns on me that for me to win, my new friend would have to lose.

'**Me, win? No way, José!** I'd never hear the end of it! Do you know how much stick I'd get from my big brothers for being such a goody-goody?' She spreads her wings out as wide as they will stretch. 'Like, this much. Now come on ... let's start by getting full marks on our assignment. The kitchen's this way.' Batz turns and swooshes out of the bathroom. 'It's a dead cert there's gonna be some grub in there,' she calls. 'Tarquin, the dude who lives here, loves his food. All we need to do is eat some, and blame it on Fluffy.'

'Who's Fluffy?' I say, leaping down from the toilet and racing along the corridor after her. She flits across the kitchen and hangs herself on the end of a wire rack. I skid across the slippery floor after her.

'Fluffy is Tarquin's cat,' says Batz casually.

My senses suddenly go into overdrive. My nose goes crazy. My whiskers stand on end. All my muscles tense. I have never seen a cat, but I know what one is – it's inbuilt into all mice.

'What's wrong with you?' asks Batz. 'Why are you shaking?'

'A CAT! A CAT LIVES HERE????' I exclaim.

'Whoa! Mega mouse meltdown,' she laughs. 'Don't worry about Fluffy. She's out hunting. Right now, I reckon she's round the back of the old petrol station, terrorising the rabbits. Dr Krapotkin hates cats too, so if we frame Fluffy, we'll definitely get full marks. Ooh, look!' she says, pointing to a box on which is written in large yellow letters:

VEGAN CRUNCHY BAR MULTIPACK
Packed full of scrummy fruits, nuts and seeds

My mouth starts to water. I realise I haven't eaten properly for several nights. I suddenly feel hungry, so hungry it hurts. But I can't possibly ... I mean, actually opening a packet ... If there were some crumbs on the floor that would be fine, but ...

'Come on! What are you waiting for? The flies-on-the-wall are watching,' whispers Batz, subtly pointing a wing in the direction of two houseflies on the wall behind us. 'Do you want to beat that rat or not?'

It's all I need to hear. I tear open the box and drag out a bar. I rip off the wrapper and WOMPH ... My nose is filled with the delicious smell of raisins and maple syrup. I take one bite, and then another, and another, and another ...

Batz tries a tiny bit and makes a 'yuk' face, then watches me devour the rest. 'Wow, you really were hungry. Come on, grab that packet and follow me. We gotta find Fluffy's bed!'

I dash after her as she zooms into the living room. I glance around, looking for clues as to where Fluffy might sleep. The left-hand cushion of the sofa is covered in fine white hair – this must be it.

I've always wondered what cats smell like and now I know: wood, smoke and death. The scent sends shudders down my spine. I'm overcome by the urge to flee.

'Come on, let's go,' I say, depositing the empty packet

before leaping off the sofa and sprinting back across the living room.

'You sure can shift when you want to!' giggles Batz, swooping after me.

But just as we get into the hallway, there's a loud **CREEEEEAK** as the bedroom door swings open ...

TARQUIN, HE POOED

Before I can hide, Tarquin steps out of the bedroom, right in front of me. If I'd been any closer, he'd have stood on me. He turns and stumbles sleepily towards the bathroom, **rubbing his enormous beard** with one hand and **scratching his bottom** with the other.

116

I glance up, looking for Batz, and glimpse a black blur disappearing into the bathroom. Moments later, Tarquin goes in too, and with a flick of his heel he kicks the bathroom door shut behind him.

I hear the sound of the toilet seat being lowered – he's about to have a poo. This could take a while.

For a second everything goes silent and then ...

'Bibbidi-bobbidi-poo!' I hear him sing. 'Bibbidi-bobbidi, bibbidi-bobbidi, bibbidi-bobbidi poo-ooo-ooo!'

SINGING? Who sings while taking a poo? And who has their own special poo song about doing one?

Finally, the poo song stops, there's a loud splash, and I hear the toilet flushing. Seconds later, Tarquin comes out and disappears back to his bedroom.

I sprint into the bathroom and find Batz hanging on the shower rail, hidden among the folds of the plastic curtain, her wings wrapped tightly round her nose.

'Maximum trauma!' she blurts. 'I wish I could un-see what I just saw. It's like he pooped a brick. It was epic. I swear half the water jumped out of the toilet when it hit. It must have weighed a ton, a humungous seed-filled whopper, a monster nut burger. Eurgh! Eurgh! Eurgh!'

Luckily, Batz's suffering was worth it. We get top marks – 20 Golden Points – for framing Fluffy. Dr Krapotkin really does hates cats, and Fluffy in particular – apparently, Fluffy ate her first husband.

Maximus also gets top marks, for doing a wee on the TV plug so that the electrics blew. Or at least he would have got full marks. Unfortunately for him, he accidentally left a few little droppings there too. If it wasn't for the fly-on-the-wall's clean-up job, Nuke-A-Pest could have been called in.

Dr Krapotkin looks very grave. 'I'm afraid I'll have to deduct your points again, darlink – we can't have Nuke-A-Pest called, not under any circumstances.'

Maximus is so furious he looks like he might explode. As he storms passed me, he viciously yanks a clump of my fur out.

'**ow!**' I squeak, but no one else sees.

The class gathers round the blackboard as we watch Dr Krapotkin tally up the scores on the leaderboard.

'And there you have it, darlinks!' she says.

I gasp.

'You can do it! **You can do it!**' says Batz bashing me excitedly with her wing.

I can't believe it. I'm in second place, only two points away. I could actually win! I turn to look at Maximus, but he's gone — I guess he must be in a really big huff. Ha!

'I must say, I've never seen a

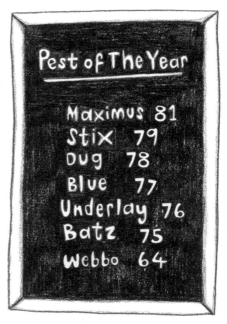

Pest of The Year

Maximus 81
Stix 79
Dug 78
Blue 77
Underlay 76
Batz 75
Webbo 64

newcomer perform like this, and so late in the year,' says
Dr Krapotkin. 'Well done, Stix. Now off to bed, everyone. It's
our visiting professor's assignment tomorrow – your final
test – and it's going to be a big night. So make sure you all
get a good day's sleep.'

MAXIMUS CUNNING

But I don't sleep well at all. All day I hear strange noises – the sound of chewing and tearing, and high-pitched laughter. I can't tell if I am awake or dreaming.

When I do finally wake, I immediately sense that something's wrong. I hear Dr Krapotkin's voice. She sounds upset and angry, and if I'm not mistaken, I can hear Maximus too.

I dash across the floor to the wardrobe, eager to see what's going on. Maybe Maximus has done something bad again and is getting more points deducted? Whatever it is,

Dr Krapotkin sounds **REALLY** cross.

I scamper up the lampshade and jump down into the wardrobe and that's when I see it.

Dr Krapotkin's shoebox has been ripped to shreds.

Teeny tiny shreds.

She turns and stares at me, accusingly. 'This is really most out of character, Stix,' she says, shaking her head.

'And you were doing so well.'

'W—w—what?' I stammer. 'No ... no! It wasn't me ... I wouldn't ... I couldn't ... I didn't! **I promise** ...'

I look at Dr Krapotkin. Surely she can't think I did this?

'It's no use denying it, mouse,' says Maximus. 'There's some of your fur right here. It must have come out while you were tearing it up — just like you tore up that box the other day.'

Sure enough, there, scattered amongst the shredded cardboard, is some of my fur.

And that's when I remember — Maximus yanking out a clump before he left last night. My heart sinks — of course! How could I be so stupid?

I've been framed. But no one will believe me if I say it now.

'I am afraid, Stix, for this heinous and regrettable crime,' says Dr Krapotkin fixing me with her small eye, 'I will be deducting your 20 Golden Points from yesterday. I'm sorry, darlink, but I can't let you get away with this. Fun is fun, but remember rule number 5 — never go too far.'

Behind her, Maximus lets out a silent cheer.

And then the reality hits me.

I've just lost 20 points. And there's only one more assignment.

I've just lost any chance I ever had of getting Maximus back.

I can never catch him now.

My plan has failed.

It's over.

BIG POINTS AND HUGE SURPRISES

I feel like giving up and going home, and I probably would if I had a home to go to. But I don't. P.E.S.T.S. is all I have.

I don't just feel bad because I've lost and Maximus has won. I feel bad because I can tell that everyone thinks I actually did it.

Everyone apart from Batz. 'I know it wasn't you,' she says, wrapping a wing round me and giving me a little hug. That makes me feel a tiny bit better, but the hurt of knowing that horrible rat has won and I've let down my grandma still stings.

'Now, darlinks,' says Dr Krapotkin, 'the time has come for our ever so special visiting professor to set us a most fantastic final challenge. So, without further ado, if you would please form an orderly queue, I shall lead you to his current residence.'

'Bring it on!' I hear Maximus snarl.

He shoots me a smug smile as he shoves his way to the front of the queue, sliding down the lampshade and out of the wardrobe. He follows right behind Dr Krapotkin as she leads us across the basement.

The further we go, the dustier and darker the basement gets. Finally, we reach a dented and ancient-looking microwave. Amazingly, it seems from the light on the display to still be working. Not only working, in fact, but — in use. The timer is ticking down: **9, 8, 7 ...**

'Coo-eee,' calls Dr Krapotkin, neatening her feathers with her good foot. 'Professor, it is I, Lyudmila Krapotkin ...'

6, 5, 4 ...

'I have the young ones here. We're all VERY excited to meet you.'

3, 2, 1 ...

There is a loud PING and the microwave door flies open.

Thick smoke bellows out. We all take a step backwards, coughing and covering our mouths.

At last, the fog clears, revealing a very strange-looking insect.

'Ooh,' I hear Dr Krapotkin sigh excitedly to herself, 'he's all the cockroach I imagined!'

The cockroach appears to have very recently been on fire. His shell is lightly smoking. One of his antennae has been badly singed and his left eye is twitching madly.

'1900 watts of pure pleasure!' he declares. 'Nothing like a good dose of radiation to start the evening.'

'My hero!' mutters Dr Krapotkin.

'Mazzzively awkzzz,' buzzes Blue, and rolls his eyes.

'Howcanshelikesuchanuglybug?' gabbles Underlay.

In one huge jump the cockroach springs up on top of the microwave. He spreads out all four of his hairy arms and declares, 'ALL HAIL THE MIGHTY PROFESSOR ARMAGEDDON!'

He stares down at us. I'm not quite sure what he's expecting, but then Dr Krapotkin begins clapping, encouraging us to join in.

'Oh, you are too kind,' booms the professor, gesturing for us to clap louder.

'Thank you, thank you,' he continues, clearly very much enjoying himself. 'Now, I have come here to your smelly – I mean, smashing – basement to announce this year's extra special, extra dangerous final challenge. And because this year's challenge is **extra dangerous**, I'm going to assign a few extra points for it too.'

'Sweet! I could really do with some bonus poin-o-las,' says Webbo.

'Amazzzzzing!' buzzes Blue.

'So, this year I have decided that the winner will receive not 20 but **50 GOLDEN POINTS!'**

Everyone, including Dr Krapotkin, lets out a shocked gasp.

I can't believe it. I can't believe my luck! If only I can win this challenge, I'll have 109 points. That's way more than Maximus's current score of 81. I still have a chance to beat him. **I CAN STILL DO IT!!!!!**

'And winning this award —' smiles Professor Armageddon '— is really ever so simple. All you have to do is make the mans' lives ... a LIVING HELL! The one who bothers them out of their tiny minds, the one who torments them to the point they can no longer cope, will be the winner. And I don't want any of this silly secretive business —' he says, narrowing his eyes, '— I want them to KNOW it was US that did it!'

There's an uncomfortable silence in the room. Batz and I exchange a horrified look. This is clearly not the P.E.S.T.S. way.

'Er ... most honorable professor,' says Dr Krapotkin, shuffling uncomfortably on her one good foot, 'um ... you know what a big fan I am of anarchic behaviour, but er... what about rule 1: a good pest should be heard but never seen? And, um, rule 4: a good pest covers its tracks?'

'Why should we cower away in our corners?' rages Professor Armageddon, pacing wildly on top of his microwave, waving his four arms dramatically. 'What have we got to be ashamed of? Nothing, apart from our own shame! Let us not hide away any more!'

'**Yeah!**' says Maximus, punching the air.

I look around at my fellow classmates and realise, to my horror, they seem to be buying it. Even shy Dug is nodding his head in agreement.

'But, Professor,' continues Dr Krapotkin, 'what about rule 3 — bother but do no harm? We're not supposed to ever go that far. How can you justify—'

'Dr Krapotkin,' says Professor Armageddon, his voice quiet now, tears filling his eyes, 'haven't we as much right to live as they?' He jumps down from the microwave and approaches her, taking her wing. 'Why do we let them terrorise us? Do we not **deserve** to live too, Dr Krapotkin?'

I look to our teacher and see to my horror that tears are forming in her eyes. 'Call me, Lyudmylla, please ...' she says with a shy smile. 'I mean, I suppose, when you put it like that. I was only saying—'

'Saying that this is our time? That this is the hour of the PEST?'

The class all clap wildly.

'Well, yes, yes, I suppose so,' says Dr Krapotkin, wiping a tear away with her wing. 'I only worry that ... perhaps, dear Professor, we could have a private chat in the wardrobe, just to clarify a few things, set my silly mind at rest?'

'Yes, yes, whatever,' sighs Professor

Armageddon. 'Why don't you go there now and I will meet you when I'm done here.'

Dr Krapotkin looks unsure, but relents and flutters off to the wardrobe to wait for him.

'Now,' shouts the professor, 'are we ready to go out there and take what's rightfully ours? To cause some serious havoc?'

'**Yes!**' screams the whole of P.E.S.T.S. in unison.

'This is crazy,' I whisper, shuffling next to Batz. 'We can't terrorise the mans like this. It's too dangerous; it doesn't make any sense. If they know we're to blame, they'll just call Nuke-A-Pest, won't they?'

'Yeah, I know,' says Batz, giving me a worried look. 'My great-great-grandpa used to say, never trust a cockroach. This dude is completely off his rocker.'

'**Now GO!**' booms Professor Armageddon. 'I want to hear screams of fear, howls of horror. The flies-on-the-walls will be watching your performance and reporting back to me. Do not let me down ...' He grins menacingly. 'Oh, and, rat,' he says, 'a word before you go.'

A moment later, everyone has disappeared, except a

smug-looking Maximus, who follows Professor Armageddon round to the side of the microwave.

Batz and I exchange a look. We are not going anywhere. What does Professor Armageddon want with Maximus? We're going to stay to find out.

THE BIG STINK!

We find the perfect hiding place
behind a large book that
has fallen off the shelf
above.

We peek over it, watching as Professor Armageddon shows Maximus a large yellow Post-it Note stuck to the side of the microwave. On the note is scribbled a very complicated-looking diagram.

'What is it?' I whisper to Batz.

'Beats me!' she mouths.

'Now,' Professor Armageddon grins, picking up a matchstick, 'stage one of my plan is in motion. And you, rat, have the honour of carrying out stage two.'

'Oh, thank you, sir!' says Maximus, beaming.

'You live in the sewers beneath the building, is that right?'

'Yes, sir.'

'You know their layout?'

'Of course, sir,' snorts Maximus.

'You know the drain cover just behind the microwave?'

'It's the way I get home every day, sir.'

'**Excellent!**' replies Professor Armageddon. 'I want you to dig a tunnel from the drain under the basement, here –' he traces a line along the diagram with the match – 'all the way to the septic tank – or "poop tank", as I believe that annoying teacher of yours calls it – HERE. He points to a large rectangular shape on the diagram.

'When poop ferments in the tank, it produces methane. I want this tunnel to be wide enough so that a large amount of this foul-smelling gas can travel quickly and efficiently along it.'

'Er, OK. But why, sir? It sounds kind of gross.'

'Why?' says Professor Armageddon, clearly not expecting to be questioned, 'because ... because I want the mans to choke on their stinky-poo gas. I want to gas them out of the block. That's why. Ha! Ha! Ha!'

'Ha! Ha! Ha!' laughs Maximus. 'And if I do that, I get 50 points.'

'Yes, yes, of course,' says the professor, rolling his eyes.

Maximus punches the air.

'Now I need you to get to work straight away,' the professor continues. 'When it comes to committing the most pestilential act there has ever been, there is no time to lose!' He throws his head back and lets out the craziest laugh I have ever heard (even crazier than Batz's). 'Now I must go and sort out this pigeon problem. Are you clear on what you have to do?'

'Yes, sir, yes!' says Maximus.

'Then DO IT,' he says, leaping off the microwave and disappearing off in the direction of the wardrobe.

'That sure is some mad plan' says Batz.

'Uh-huh,' I nod, 'we don't want to drive the mans out and we sure don't want him winning all the points. We've got to stop him.'

'Too right,' nods Batz.

But by the time we get to the drain cover we find it open and Maximus already disappeared inside.

I peer in. All I can see is a long drop, and then black. A strong smell of dirty water hits my nose, the kind you find in a washing-up bowl that's not been emptied for a long time.

'Maximus!' I call out in a loud whisper, but I can't see him in the darkness. 'We'd better follow him,' I say to Batz.

'You first!' she says with a

grin. 'You mice are good at this kind of
thing.'

   I am about to leap down when
a voice from below booms, **'Mice
are good at nothing!'**

   Maximus appears
beneath us. 'What do
you morons want?'

'We heard what Professor Armageddon asked you to do,' I say as boldly as I can, 'and ... and we've come to tell you it's a really bad idea. I mean, driving the mans out of the block. That's not good. Can't you see he's using you to do his dirty work? You shouldn't do it.'

'Oh, I get it,' grins Maximus. 'I see what you muppets are doing. You're trying to stop me getting all the Golden Points so you can get them all yourself. What do you take me for, a **brainless goon?'**

'Well ... now you come to mention it ...' laughs Batz.

Maximus narrows his eyes. 'If only the Plagues were here, I'd set them on your pathetic little hairy bottoms – bite them to bits. But sadly they're off biting that stupid mans baby. I've sent them off to maximise our terrorising – really impress the professor. You have no idea the nasty diseases they carry.'

'You've sent them to bite Boo-Boo?' I gasp.

'If that's what you call that ugly crying thing that lives in Flat 3, then yes.' He sneers. 'Now if you will excuse me, I have a tunnel to dig and some points to win.'

And with that, he disappears into the darkness of the drain.

BOO-BOO, NO!

I know Boo-Boo is a mans and that I shouldn't care. But I do. I feel like in some strange way we are friends, family even. We've grown up together; we've even eaten the same food.

'I'm sorry, Batz, but Boo-Boo is **more important** to me than some silly points, and hopefully the gas won't smell THAT bad. I have to go and help her,' I say, waiting for her to call me a stupid mans fan like Maximus would. But she doesn't.

'Of course,' she says simply. 'And I'm coming with you. You take the hidden highway. I'll see you up there.'

I can't help but smile as she swoops off. 'Thank you!'

I call after her.

'Don't be daft. That's what friends are for, isn't it?'
And with a wink over her shoulder she's gone.

I dart over to the tunnels. I shudder at the thought of
poor Boo-Boo covered in large, red bites.

I scramble into the third hole along and this time I
find myself at first in the familiar foam as before, and
then a pipe. Although it slopes up steeply, the inside of it
is helpfully scored with grooves, making it easy to climb.
I frantically scramble up, following its twists and turns,
until finally I see light. I pull myself out of the pipe and
find I am sitting in the bottom of the kitchen sink. The
familiar smell of Flat 3 hits me. For a moment it stops me
in my tracks as memories flood my head. But then I hear
the swoosh of wings above me and look up to see Batz.
'You're getting faster,' she grins. 'Come on.'

Quick as a flash, **I sprint up a dirty wooden spoon**
and out of the sink. I tear across the countertop and leap
down to the floor. I'm in such a rush to get to Boo-Boo that
I almost don't notice Trevor. He's fast asleep as ever, back
from the vet's now, and sporting a flashy new red collar.

I tiptoe past him and sprint up the stairs to Boo-Boo's bedroom.

As we enter the room, I hear the unmistakable high-pitched giggle of the Plagues.

'It looks well juicy,' says Plague One.

'Yeah,' says Plague Two. 'Where shall we bite first?'

'**Stop!**' I shout, bounding across the room and up on to the cot. 'Please don't bite her, please.'

'Who invited you to the feast?' laughs Plague One as he crawls around on Boo-Boo's face.

She whimpers and scratches at him, unaware of what's bothering her.

'You shouldn't do this,' I reply. 'It's wrong. You're doing harm. You'll hurt her, make her itch, make her sick. Can't you hear how upset she is?'

'The prof says we can do what we like now!' says Plague Two, poking his head out from an armhole of Boo-Boo's Babygro. 'And we like to BITE!'

'Watch out, Stix ...' cries Batz suddenly.

I hear a low growl from the doorway. My whiskers twitch wildly as I turn to see Trevor entering the room, bearing all his teeth.

'Mouse!'
He barks, leaping towards me.
'I smell you. I was waiting for you to come back. Mouse is back! Mouse is back! Come quick!'
'Shhhhhh, shhhhhh,' I beg him. 'Listen,

Trevor, I know you think mice are bad, but I came to protect Boo-Boo, I promise! There are two fleas and they are going to bite her ... please help us!'

Trevor stops barking, and lets out a low, rumbling growl. 'What? Fleas? Where?!'

My whiskers pick up movement again. It's the mans; they've heard Trevor! I look at him, at his shiny red collar and suddenly I know what we have to do.

'Your collar, Trevor! It's a flea collar, right?'

'Uh-oh,' I hear the Plagues say in unison.

Trevor pauses for a moment, thinking hard. Then, as if suddenly realising my point, he growls and leaps up to the cot, pushing his neck and collar right over it.

'Trevor HATE fleas. Go away, EVIL fleas.'

'URGH! URGH!' the Plagues cry. 'INSECTICIDE! PROPOXUR! DEATH!

147

DEATH! GET IT AWAY! GET IT AWAY!' They leap out of the cot like it's on fire. In a few giant leaps they are out of the door and gone.

'Stix, you gotta hide,' cries Batz from the doorway. 'Mans incoming! And he's got a, er ... toilet brush in his hand.' She swoops across the room and hides herself behind one of Boo-Boo's large fluffy toys.

'Ickle mush!' I hear a small voice say. I look up and see Boo-Boo peering down at me through the bars of her cot. I smile for a second, forgetting the danger. She really is so cute! 'Hewow ickle mush, you back!'

'What's going on, Trevor? Whoever's there ... you should know, I've got a ... very prickly bog brush and I'm not afraid to use it!' calls MyLove and a second later he bursts into the room.

And that's it. It's too late. I'm stuck, standing on the edge of the baby's cot, like it's me that's about to bite her. The second I move, he'll see me. But if I don't, and stay where I am, he'll see me too ... **My body freezes**, just like it did before.

Trevor looks at me, then runs to MyLove. 'No mouse,

Trevor wrong,' he barks. '**Back to bed! Back to bed!**'

But, of course, all MyLove hears is 'BARK! BARK! BARK!'

'Mush! Mush come me!' cries Boo-Boo, holding her hand out. 'Me give mush cudwle.'

'Boo-Boo?' MyLove's voice is worried as he approaches. 'Boo-Boo honey, who are you talking t—'

I'm done for. I know it. He's going to see me. There's only one thing I can do. One thing that might stop Nuke-A-Pest coming back and doing a Double Whammy on the whole building. One thing that can save my new friends.

Quick as a flash, I fall to the floor.

As if Trevor's got me. As if I'm ...

Dead.

DMD2

Everything is happening so fast I hardly have time to think. I try to remember exactly what Grandma did. My heart is beating like mad. I try desperately to slow it. *Relax, relax, I think,* as I let my tongue loll out of the side of my mouth.

'ARRGHHHHH!' screams MyLove.

'What is it?' cries Schnookums, stumbling into the room behind him.

'You won't believe it; it's a MOUSE. A DEAD mouse. AGAIN!!!!'

'Ugh, how disgusting!' says Schnookums, pushing her way past him and bundling up Boo-Boo. 'Boo-Boo darling, come with me. Trevor, out, come on. Just shut the door on it, MyLove, and call Nuke-A-Pest. We'll have to disinfect the carpet now,' she grumbles.

'Sorry, mouse,' woofs Trevor quietly. He looks over his shoulder at me as he's ushered towards the door. 'I tried.'

'Did you get the mouse, Trevor?' says MyLove, patting him on the head. 'Did you protect Boo-Boo? Well done, boy, well done.'

'Silly mans,' grumbles Trevor as he trudges out of the room. 'Why you NEVER listen?'

152

As soon as they have left the room, Batz swoops down from her hiding place. 'Stix?' she says quietly. 'Stix?!'

I sit up.

'Yikes!' she says, leaping back. 'Oh my god, Stix! **I thought you were dead!** You gave me such a fright. That was a great trick, though. Well done! Wow, you really showed those fleas and those mans, and that dog too! Wait till I tell everyone about this. Now come on, let's get out of here, before—'

'Batz,' I say, 'Batz, stop!' She pauses, looking at me questioningly. I feel a lump rise up in my throat. 'I wish I could leave. But, if I leave, they'll know I'm alive and Nuke-A-Pest will come and fumigate the place. Then it won't just be me that gets it — it'll be everyone. I have to do what Grandma did. I have to do the Dead Mouse Deception.'

Batz's eyes grow wide. 'But you're ... you're my best friend,' she pleads, 'I don't want you to get flushed!'

I can't believe she just said the words 'best friend'. Finally, just as I am about to get dropped down the loo, I find out I have a best friend. I feel my eyes start to water. Then I hear the *clomp! clomp! clomp!* of heavy footsteps coming back up the stairs.

'Go!' I say. 'Get out of here before they see you.'

'No! I can't let you do this. I—'

'I said GO!' I say, as fiercely as I can. 'Or we're ALL dead!'

Batz's faces drops as she realises I'm right. There's no other way.

'Goodbye, my friend,' she says, touching my cheek gently with her wing, her eyes full of tears. 'I'll make sure everyone knows how brave you are ...' Then, as the door handle turns, she swoops quick as a flash over to the fireplace and, with a last sad look over her shoulder, disappears up the chimney.

I resume my 'dead' position just in time, eyes glazed, tongue lolling. MyLove storms back into the room. He has the phone pressed to his ear.

'It's just ringing and ringing. They're probably out on a call. Maybe it's another rogue raid, maybe we don't need them. Maybe I should just ... er ...'

'**Yeah, flush it!**' Schnookums shouts back. 'Sooner the better. Before it starts decomposing.'

My heart is pounding. Oh my god. I can't believe this is going to happen.

I fight the urge to yelp as MyLove gingerly picks me up by my tail. It takes everything I have, every fibre of strength, not to flinch, not to bite him and run.

As he carries me to the bathroom, I pass, upside down, through the happy world I once shared with Grandma. I glimpse the kitchen, the washing machine ... Oh, how I wish we were both tucked up in our nest just

155

the way we used to be.

We reach the toilet. MyLove lifts the lid. I stare down into the water below.

'Oh, hi, hello, sorry I didn't think anyone was in the office ... I'm calling from Flat 3, Peewit Mansions,' I hear him say into the phone. 'We've got another dead one; what do you think, another rogue raid?'

Yes, yes, another rogue raid. Just flush me down the toilet and think no more about it, I beg them to say.

'Uh-huh, uh-huh,' says MyLove, 'you think a full building inspection to be on the safe side, uh-huh, and the Double Whammy's still very much a possibility, Ok, thanks. We'll see you soon'.

His fingers release my tail.

NO! NO! NO! This can't be happening. They can't do an inspection; they'll find everyone! And they'll do a Double Whammy! That's not what was supposed to happen.

The water rushes towards me.

I take one last long deep breath.

I'm about to drown and it's all for ...

... nothing.

FLUSHED

The water hits me like a
punch in the face. It fills
my eyes, my ears, my
nose. For a split
second my body
bobs up to the
surface. Then a
thunderous wall of
water crashes down,
filling the toilet and
pushing me down,
down, down. My body

somersaults over and over – this is what it must feel like to be in a washing machine.

I go down, then up, then down again and then everything goes black. The water rockets me forward. My arms and legs bang against the side of something hard and plastic – I'm in a pipe. I'm trapped in a water-filled pipe. My chest starts to burn. I'm out of air. I want to breathe. I want to open my mouth, but I know I shouldn't.

Twinkly spots of bright light begin to dance in front of my eyes. I can't fight the urge any longer. I gasp. Water fills my mouth. My lungs burn. Is this how Grandma felt? Is this how it ended for her? My body loses all strength. I feel myself go limp. I no longer feel panic. I feel strangely calm. *This is it,* I say to myself.

This
is
THE END.

WOOOMPH!

I'm flung forward, out of the pipe. For a second I'm flying through air. I choke and gasp all at once. Then SPLOSH! I'm back underwater again. I paddle my legs as hard as I can. I feel my head break the surface. I cough and splutter, and water spurts from my mouth. The air around me stinks – like the smell that came out of Tarquin's bathroom the other night. I can't see a thing; it's pitch black. This must be the septic tank.

I'm alive, I realise. *I'm alive!*

And if I am alive, then is it possible ... could it be ... that Grandma is alive too?

I paddle my legs like crazy, keeping my head as far as I possibly can above the foul-smelling water.

'Grandma! Grandma!' I shout into the darkness. 'Grandma, are you here?'

I listen carefully for a reply, for a sign, for anything. But all I can hear is the sound of my own frantic breathing.

'Grandma!' I call.

I feel something long and soft pass underneath my toes

... Eurgh, was that a ...

I try not to think about it as I keep swimming around and calling as loud as I can. 'Grandma! Grandma!' I'm unable to hide the tremble in my voice. 'Grandma, please be here, please ...'

Another object nudges against my shoulder. I spin round. What just touched me? It nudges into me again. It's a big roll of soggy cardboard – a toilet roll, with all the paper gone.

Then I hear a quiet moan, and I feel, on top of the loo roll, something ... wet and furry. Something mouse-like.

'Grandma! Grandma, is that you?' I shout. 'Grandma!'

There is silence and then a cough ... and then ...

'Stix?'

'Grandma! You're alive! You're alive!' I cry.

'Just,' she croaks weakly.

I dare not put any weight on the loo roll in case I sink it. Instead I paddle next to her, gently holding one of her paws in mine.

'Oh my darling, what has brought you to this terrible place?' she whispers, squeezing my hand. 'I've tried and tried, but there's no way out of this tank. Only a way in. I'm sorry, my boy.'

'It's OK, Grandma,' I say. 'I'm with you and that's all that matters.'

'You know,' she chuckles, 'I'm not even sure if you really are here or if I'm just dreaming. I think I'm going mad. I heard another voice down here not so long ago, talking about digging a tunnel, and there was this high-pitched giggling too. But that's impossible ... I think the fumes must have gone to my head.'

The effort of paddling is making my breathing heavy. I take another gulp of foul-smelling air. And that's when it hits me.

Grandma's not going crazy.

It was Maximus, digging his tunnel.

'No, Grandma, you're not mad,' I say. 'I know who was down here ... It's that rat, Maximus, the one that was in our kitchen ... He was sent down here to dig a tunnel, a tunnel from the septic tank back to the drain underneath the basement. We have to find it. That's our way out!'

I can tell Grandma is confused, but I don't have time

to explain. I fan out my whiskers and slowly spin myself round, trying to detect the slightest breeze. I get the faintest of tickles; it's coming from straight ahead. Using my nose, I nudge Grandma and her soggy loo roll forward. There it is again ... this time a little stronger. I paddle some more. Now I am getting a hint of rat scent.

With a soggy splodge the roll hits the wall of the tank. I run my paws along the cold plastic, and then I feel it — a rough, gnawed edge.

'That's it!' I cry. 'I've found it. I've found the way out! Can you walk?' I ask nervously — there is no way I am strong enough to carry a soggy grandma.

'Don't you worry about me, boy! I've been in worse spots than this ...' With a groan she eases herself off the roll. We wriggle through the hole, out of the septic tank, to freedom ...

PONGY PIPES

As we hurry down the tunnel back to the basement, I fill Grandma in on **everything** that's happened – about leaving the flat, about P.E.S.T.S., about Maximus, about Professor Armageddon's mad plan.

She looks at me with a mix of curiosity and shock.

'We'll have a little chat about your utter lack of caution later, shall we?' she says. I think, I hope, **I detect a small smile**.

She's slow at first, but with every step she takes, she seems to find more strength. 'If the situation is as dire as you say, if this Professor Armageddon is endangering the life of both pests and mans, then we need to get help,' she says. 'We need to call in the Council of Pests; they'll put a halt to this nonsense immediately. No one disobeys the C.O.P.s!'

'But how will we get to them, this council, where are they?'

'Don't you worry,' she says, tapping her nose. 'I'll deal with that. You just get us out of this tunnel. The smell in here is **disgusting**.'

At last we reach the end of the tunnel, and find ourselves in a much larger concrete pipe. I stop for a moment and let my whiskers feel the air.

'The drain beneath the basement!' I say, and, sure enough, up ahead I see a faint semi-circle of light – the drain cover! And it's been left **half open!**

Using what short claws I have, I begin

to climb the wall of the concrete pipe towards the opening. I'm almost at the top when a familiar face appears.

'**Batz!**' I shout.

'Stix!' whispers Batz. 'You're alive! You're alive! I managed to get the drain cover a little open, just in case. Oh, this is the best thing EVER! I thought I would never see you again. I thought you were dead. I thought you drowned, I thought— **Wow, you smell gross,** is that the smell of—'

'Batz,' I say, interrupting her, 'can you ...'

'Oh yeah, sorry,' says Batz, giving me a hand out of the hole.

'I need you to help me get my grandma out too,' I say with a smile.

'What?!' says Batz, breaking into a huge smile. 'Your grandma's alive too? Holy moly! **Jeepers creepers** ... Hi, Stix's grandma!'

We've just managed to get Grandma out of the drain when we hear a booming shout from behind us. 'Mouse!' It's Professor Armageddon. He's spotted me. 'Mouse, is that you? Come over here and show yourself! Our hero of the day!'

Grandma crouches down out of sight. 'Go!' she whispers. 'I'll be back with the C.O.P.s as quick as I can.'

'MOUSE!' cries Professor Armageddon again. 'Come on, get over here!'

I nervously make my way round to the front of the microwave; there isn't time to say goodbye.

'Here he is!' says the professor, excitedly waving his four hairy arms at me. 'The star of the class! The flies-on-the-wall in Flat 3 have informed me that thanks to this mouse making himself seen, Nuke-A-Pest are on their way right now.'

'Nuke-A-Pest!' everyone gasps.

'For this incredible achievement I award our mouse here the full 50 Golden Points! I have no doubt that this will make you the Pesty of the Year, or whatever your silly award is called.'

'WHAT? THOSE POINTS ARE MINE!' screams Maximus. 'YOU CAN'T!'

'Of course I can,' laughs Professor Armageddon. 'I can do whatever I like!'

I can't believe it. I've done it. **I've won**. But it doesn't feel like a victory. In fact, it feels the opposite. I've helped crazy Professor Armageddon with his insane plan.

'Now, I can see some of you are a little concerned about Nuke-A-Pest,' he grins, 'but there really is no need. You see, thanks to clever me, there will soon be no Nuke-A-Pest at all. Because while our little mouse here has carried out stage three of my master plan by summoning them here, the rat has been carrying out stage two. He's dug a tunnel from the septic tank to just under the basement ... **can you smell that gas**, that highly flamable gas seeping out from the drain cover?

Everyone gasps again, and looks over to the drain cover.

The gas is coming out so thick and fast now, you can almost see it.

'Er, you never said anything about it being flammable,' says Maximus, sounding alarmed. 'You tricked me!'

'Well, here's a life lesson for you ...' cackles Dr Armageddon. '**Never trust a cockroach.**'

'Told you', whispers Batz.

I can't believe it. We should have guessed his plan would be bigger than just some stinky gas.

'Now all that's left is for stage four – make a spark and blow this mansion block sky high! All hail the craziest, most cunning cockroach ever. My parents said I'd never amount to anything, no better than a pathetic woodlouse, they said. Well, Mummy and Daddy, now I'm about to blow up a whole building. How's that for over-achieving? I'll soon be so famous you'll be learning about me in your lessons,' he says, grinning wildly at us. 'Oh, sorry ... no you won't. Because you will be blown up too! Ha! Ha! Ha! Ha!'

ARMAGEDDON

I glance around, frantically looking for Dr Krapotkin. But our teacher is nowhere to be seen. We are all alone. It's down to us to do something.

'You can't do this,' I shout. 'You can't kill us all.'

The professor eyes me in stony silence. From a tatty suitcase leaning up against the bookshelf comes a muffled cry. The suitcase rocks violently from side to side, then topples over. Its catch pings open and a **very angry Dr Krapotkin tumbles out**.

'This is wrong! You mustn't do it!' she blusters. 'Oh, I never should have trusted you ... But the way you looked at me ...'

'Hush now, Krapotkin. Don't get your feathers in a flap,' laughs Professor Armageddon. 'There really is no need to worry. This will soon be over. All I need to do now is toss this —' he reveals a ball of tinfoil in one of his claws '— into my lovely microwave. Then, when I press COOK, the microwave's electromagnetic waves will hit the free electrons on the foil's metallic surface, causing them to move rapidly from side to side, thus creating a SPARK – see? They don't call me professor for nothing!' He beams and turns to face the class. 'And who knows what happens when you expose flammable gas to a flame or spark?'

Dug's hand shoots up. 'It creates an explosion?' he says.

'**correctamundo, mole. KABOOM!** I'm going to blow this place sky high.'

'But you'll die just like us!' blurts Dr Krapotkin.

'Actually, no,' smiles Professor Armageddon. 'I mean, yes, you will all die. But we cockroaches, we can survive anything ... even a nuclear attack. I'm afraid you're what they call "collateral damage". I guess you could say you are the price of my success! Ha! Ha! Ha!

'Ooh, and what's this?' he continues, cocking his head to one side. I hear the faint screech of tyres coming from somewhere above ground. 'The sound of Nuke-A-Pest's van arriving! Now to kick off the final phase of my master plan...' He tosses the ball of foil into the microwave. 'All I need is to press COOK. Shall we count down together?'

I look around desperately. Where's Grandma? Where are the C.O.P.s? We're running out of time.

Everyone starts to panic. Maximus and Plague descend into a fierce argument about how stupid he has been. Dug dashes off and burrows himself into a pile of old newspapers. Blue goes buzzing mad.

Underlay goes into chewing overdrive, nervously destroying her comfort carpet. Webbo starts frantically spinning a protective web round himself.

'You silly fools,' Professor Armageddon laughs. 'There's nowhere to hide. Accept your fate, embrace the end, die with pride—'

My ears suddenly prick up. Is that ...? Yes, it is. It's the faint sound of singing, drifting down the hidden highway.

'Bibbidi-bobbidi-bibbidi-bibbidi ...'

'Smile ... be happy corpses,' continues Professor Armageddon gleefully.

I glance up at Batz and catch her eye. 'Tarquin,' we whisper in unison. My ears pick up another sound. It starts as a faint rattle, but soon it's a roar, travelling across the ceiling towards us. It can only be the sound of one thing.

The poop pipe!

POOMAGEDDON

'Holy salmonella outbreak, what's that awful din?' shouts Professor Armageddon.

I glance up at the inspection cap. It's directly above the microwave. **This is it. This is our chance.** And if it's a Tarquin poo in the pipe, then it's going to be a big one. I can see Batz is thinking the same.

'We need to get up there,' I mouth, 'and loosen the cap ...'

Batz nods. She silently flits over to the cap and pushes with all her might, but it won't come loose. She's not strong enough.

I need to help her. But how am I going to get that high?

There's only one thing for it. I am going to have to pull off the most amazing Stix Steeplechase ever.

I glance around, quickly formulating my route.

CHAIR LEG > LAMP CORD > INSPECTION CAP.

I only have time for two deep breaths. I hope this doesn't make me any less lucky!

Quick as a flash, I sprint to the stack of chairs and begin to scrabble up a rusty metal leg.

'What are you doing, mouse? Hiding up there's not going to save you,' I hear Professor Armageddon cackle over the roar of the pipe.

I hear it shudder above me. I've got to go faster or whatever's inside is going to pass straight over us.

'Right, enough of this silly nonsense,' booms the professor. 'It's time to get on with the show. Let the countdown begin ...'

I skid across the chair's ripped plastic seat and I glance towards the pipe. Batz is poised ready to go..

'THREE ...'

I reach the edge of the chair and hurl myself at the lampshade cord. I grab it between my paws. It swings me up towards the ceiling, towards the inspection cap.

'TWO ...'

I can barely hear Professor Armageddon's voice over the thundering rush of water.

I let go of the cord and whip my tail, using it to propel me forward. Batz swoops towards the opposite side of the cap. For a brief moment, flying through the air ... I am a wingless bat.

'ONE!'

BOMPH! We hit the cap, hard. I feel it shift and then, **BINGO!** Off it falls. And I'm falling too, spinning and spinning through the air until I land with a thud in front of the professor. The cap falls a second after me. It hits him squarely in the middle of the head and dings off, just as he's about to press the button of the microwave.

It startles him for a moment, but then he looks down at me and smirks. 'Is that all you've got? Bad luck, mouse. Nothing gets through this exoskeleton.' He taps his shell. 'Hard as nails.'

But it's not over yet.

'Bibbidi-bobbidi-pooooo-oooo-ooooooooooooo!' sings Tarquin.

I look up to see the tip of an enormous poo appear from the pipe.

'Anyway, time's up!' says the professor, his finger hovering over the button. 'It's time to blow up this building and prove once and for all that we cockroaches ...'

I've never seen a poo so large in all my life. It escapes from the pipe and begins to plummet.

'... are totally, utterly, one hundred per cent invincibl—' WUMP!

The poo squashes him flat.

'Holy granola, Tarquin the pooper's done it!' laughs Batz.

The basement explodes into cheers. Batz swoops down next to me and together we inspect the poo. It's full of tiny bits of nuts. 'Professor Armageddon didn't SEED that one coming. HEE! HA! HA! HEE!'

But before I can reply, from out of nowhere a swarm of ants pours into the basement, led by Grandma. They come from everywhere: the ceiling, the air vents, the cracks in the walls, every nook and cranny.

'EVERYBODY DOWN!' declares

the largest of the ants. 'CODE RED! WE'RE LOOKING FOR A
ROGUE ROACH ON THE RAMPAGE. I REPEAT, CODE RED.'

'He's under that enormo-poop!' giggles Batz, 'so ...
shouldn't that be a code BROWN?' She throws a wing round
me and laughs hysterically. Everyone else rolls their eyes,
but I can't help but **laugh along with my best friend.**

PEST OF THE YEAR

Dr Krapotkin gathers us all into the wardrobe. We all celebrate as we hear the sound of Nuke-A-Pest's van screeching away.

Behind us, the C.O.P.s roll the giant poo off Professor Armageddon. It takes all their strength. He's been squashed flat, but amazingly is still alive.

'**Good riddance!**' says Dr Krapotkin, dabbing at her eyes as they carry him off, thin as a piece of paper.

'Dear Lyudmylia, you poor thing, whatever did he do to you?' says Grandma, placing a caring paw on Dr Krapotkin's even more battered right wing.

'Oh, you know, Hazel, my darlink ... nothing this old pigeon can't shake off,' she says, ruffling her feathers.

'I believed him for a moment, he was so charming, but when I expressed my doubts, he turned on me ... I should have known better!'

'You two know each other?' I ask, looking between Grandma and Dr Krapotkin. It's unbelievable – how many more things about Grandma don't I know?

'Oh, yes,' laughs Dr Krapotkin. 'We go back a very long way. Remember the Great Fridge Raid of Flat 1?'

'I've never seen anyone eat a loaf of bread so fast!' Grandma howls with laughter.

'Now, darlinks, and visiting alumni,' says Dr Krapotkin, with a nod to Grandma, 'as is customary after the final challenge, it is time to tot up the Golden Points and award Pest of the Year.' She turns to the leaderboard. 'Now, Maximus, I am afraid, darlink, that after that whole tunnel-digging, siding-with-a-maniac thing, I will be stripping you of all your points.'

Maximus doesn't say a word. He just sits there, glowering at his toes. The Plagues, for once, are silent too.

'So, Stix, given the 50 points Professor Armageddon awarded you, that would make you—'

'I don't want them, Miss,' I say. 'They were points given for doing something bad.'

'I'm very glad to hear you say that,' says Dr Krapotkin. 'It is very mature of you, darlink. I think we've all learned a lot of lessons here today – myself included.'

Grandma smiles at me proudly, and gives my hand a little squeeze.

'And I am afraid, brave and heroic though yours and Batz's actions were, they happened after the final challenge, so I can't award any points for them. Rules are rules!'

'Phew!' says Batz under her breath.

'In which case,' says Dr Krapotkin with a smile, 'it gives me great pleasure to announce that the winner of Pest of the Year is ...'

She swivels her head, looking at us one at a time.

'**DUG!**' she proclaims.

'**Hooray!**' We all clap.

Dug clamps his two huge paws to his face. 'Me, really? No way!' he says, tears tumbling down his furry cheeks. 'I've never won anything ... ever.'

'Or will again,' I hear Maximus mutter nastily under his breath.

'Shut up, loozzzer,' buzzes Blue.

'Yeah, button it, Twerpimus,' laughs Webbo.

'Gobacktoyourstinkysewerandnevercomeback!' gabbles Underlay fiercely through her tiny chunk of remaining comfort carpet.

After everyone has congratulated Dug and said their goodbyes till next term, there's nothing left to do but return to Flat 3. It's going to feel strange being back there, but I'm looking forward to it in a way. There's just one thing I need to find out before I go. Something I've been desperate to know but too scared to ask.

'Grandma,' I say, trying to hide the nerves in my voice, 'I've been ... er ... thinking ... about P.E.S.T.S. ... and wondering ...'

The words get stuck in my throat.

'If you can still go next term?' offers Grandma.

I nod eagerly.

'I've been thinking about that too,' she sighs. 'I had a funny feeling this time would come, what with you going out every night while I slept, gallivanting around.'

I can't believe it. She knew all along! My grandma really is full of surprises.

'I thought after what happened to your parents, if I kept you home, with me, I could keep you safe. But I can see I was wrong. To be a truly rounded mouse you need more than just your old grandma ...'

'So, I can ...?' I can hardly bring myself to say the words.

'How can I say no?' she says, hugging me tightly.

'Woo-hoo!' cries Batz, swooping down and giving me a high-five. I can't believe she was eavesdropping all along!

'But on one condition,' says Grandma. 'You keep that little nose of yours out of any more danger!'

'Of course, Grandma,' I say as solemnly as I can. 'No more crazy adventures for me.'

'**Hee! Ha! Ha! Hee!**' laughs Batz. '**That's a good one!**'

Stix and Batz, what have you drawn on my face?

When **EMER STAMP** was young she dreamed of being a vet, but she was rubbish at science. She was, however, not bad at art. So she became a graphic designer and went to work in advertising, where she became the creative director of the agency behind the John Lewis Christmas adverts. At the same time, she wrote the bestselling **DIARY OF PIG** series, and decided she liked writing books more than writing adverts. And now here she is on the back page of her new book, **PESTS**. With a moustache drawn on her face.

If you'd like to see more of Stix and the PESTS gang,
you can find them here—
PESTS website www.pestsbook.com
Emer's website www.emerstamp.com
Emer's YouTube channel The World of Emer Stamp

(Pssst... Did you find the hidden message on the edge of the book?
Check out the PESTS website for more secrets, games and all
kinds of pesty fun. But remember, it's for **PESTS ONLY!**)